CW00543060

James Hadley Chase (born Ren
born in London in 1906. He wo
which time he was inspired l
and went on to write his own thrillers and gangster stories,
also set in the United States. He first found success with
No Orchids for Miss Blandish which was published in 1939
and was one of the most successful books of the thirties,
selling several million copies. George Orwell described it as
'a brilliant piece of writing with hardly a wasted word or a
jarring note anywhere'. It was subsequently dramatised and
performed on London's West End and also made into a film.
Chase went on to gain popularity for his numerous other
gangster stories, and by the end of the war he was one of
Britain's most successful thriller writers. During his career
he produced some ninety books, also writing under the
names of James L Dochery, Ambrose Grant and Raymond
Marshall. He travelled widely, though only visited the USA
late in life. He died in 1985 whilst in Switzerland.

BY THE SAME AUTHOR
ALL PUBLISHED BY HOUSE OF STRATUS

JAMES HADLEY
CHASE

The Whiff of Money

Copyright © 1969 Hervey Raymond

All rights reserved. No part of this publication may be reproduced, stored in a retrieval system, or transmitted, in any form, or by any means (electronic, mechanical, photocopying, recording, or otherwise), without the prior permission of the publisher. Any person who does any unauthorised act in relation to this publication may be liable to criminal prosecution and civil claims for damages.

The right of James Hadley Chase to be identified as the author of this work has been asserted.

This edition published in 2000 by The House of Stratus, an imprint of Stratus Books Ltd., 21 Beeching Park, Kelly Bray, Cornwall, PL17 8QS, UK.
www.houseofstratus.com

Typeset, printed and bound by The House of Stratus.

A catalogue record for this book is available from the British Library and the Library of Congress.

ISBN 1-84232-118-8

Cover design: Marc Burville-Riley
Cover image: Photonica

This book is sold subject to the condition that it shall not be lent, re-sold, hired out, or otherwise circulated without the publisher's express prior consent in any form of binding, or cover, other than the original as herein published and without a similar condition being imposed on any subsequent purchaser, or bona fide possessor.

This is a fictional work and all characters are drawn from the author's imagination. Any resemblances or similarities to persons either living or dead are entirely coincidental.

1

On this brilliantly sunny May morning, Paris was looking at its best.

From his large office window, John Dorey, head of the French division of the Central Intelligence Agency, surveyed the trees with their fresh green foliage, the young girls in their new spring outfits and the Place de la Concorde, besieged as usual by traffic. He felt it was good to be alive. He glanced at the few files on his desk and was glad there was nothing for his immediate attention. Relaxing back in his executive chair, he contemplated the view through the window with a benign smile.

With thirty-nine years' service in Intelligence behind him, Dorey, aged sixty-six had good reason to be pleased with himself. Not only did he hold the exalted rank of Divisional Director (Paris), but he also had been practically begged to remain in office beyond the usual retiring age. This was unassailable proof that his work had been and was still beyond reproach and that he could consider himself indispensable.

Dorey was a small, birdlike man, wearing rimless spectacles. He looked more like a successful banker than what he was: the shrewd, ruthless Director of an extremely efficient organisation whose secret machinations and wealth were so vast that few people realised just how powerful it was.

As Dorey was thinking that the girl, waiting to cross the street and who was wearing a gay micro-mini dress, was the perfect picture of a spring morning, his telephone bell buzzed.

Dorey frowned. The telephone was the bane of his life. One moment he had peace and quiet: the next moment the telephone would shatter the atmosphere as nothing else could.

Lifting the receiver, he said, "Yes?"

Mavis Paul, his secretary, announced, "Captain O'Halloran on the line, sir. Shall I put him through?"

Captain Tim O'Halloran was in charge of all the CIA agents in Europe. He was not only Dorey's right hand man, but also a close friend.

Dorey sighed. Whenever O'Halloran telephoned, there was usually trouble.

"Yes ... I'll talk to him." When the line clicked, Dorey went on, "Is that you, Tim?"

"Good morning, sir." O'Halloran's gravelly voice was curt. "Would you scramble, please?"

Trouble! Dorey thought as he pressed down the scrambler button. "Okay, Tim ... what is it?"

"I've had a report phoned in by Alec Hammer ... he covers Orly airport. He tells me that Henry Sherman has just arrived off the overnight flight from New York. Sherman is wearing a disguise and travelling on a false passport."

Dorey blinked. He wondered if his hearing was failing. When you reach the age of sixty-six ...

"*Who* did you say?"

"Henry Sherman. *The* Henry Sherman."

Dorey felt a rush of blood to his head.

"Is this a joke?" he demanded, his voice sharp. "What the hell are you talking about?"

"Henry Sherman has just left Orly airport, heading for central Paris, wearing a disguise and with a false passport," O'Halloran repeated woodenly.

"I don't believe it! There must be a mistake! Sherman is in Washington! I ..."

"I know where he is *supposed* to be, sir, but right now he is on his way to the centre of Paris. Hammer is sure of this. You may remember Hammer was Sherman's bodyguard for four years before he was transferred to us. Hammer says Sherman's walk, the way he swings his arms and jerks his head are unmistakable. This man, wearing a moustache and dark glasses travelled Tourist class from New York. Hammer says this man is Henry Sherman. Hammer is one of my best men. He doesn't make mistakes."

"But Sherman is guarded night and day by the FBI! He couldn't possibly have left Washington without them knowing and we would have been alerted. Hammer must be mistaken!"

"No, sir." There was now a note of impatience in O'Halloran's voice. "And another thing: this man is travelling on Jack Cain's passport. You will remember Cain looks very much like Sherman and was used two or three times last year as a decoy to get the Press away from Sherman. Since then Cain has grown a moustache."

"Are you sure this man isn't Cain?"

"I'm sure. I've been checking. Right now, Cain is in hospital with a fractured leg from a car accident. Sherman is supposed to be in bed at his residence with flu. Only his wife sees him. No one else goes into his room. Somehow, Sherman has evaded his guards while his wife is pretending he is still in bed. I am convinced that Hammer is right: Henry Sherman is footloose in Paris."

"Do you know where he is staying?"

"No sir. Hammer lost him when Sherman took the only taxi from Orly airport. Hammer has the number of the taxi. He's waiting at Orly to see if the taxi returns so he can get a line on Sherman, but it's a long shot. Do you want me to check all the hotels?"

Dorey hesitated, his mind working swiftly. Finally, he said, "No. Did Sherman have any luggage with him?"

"A small suitcase ... that's all."

"Then leave it, Tim. Warn Hammer to say nothing. If he spots the taxi he is to try to find out where Sherman was taken, but he mustn't make a thing of it. This could be a very tricky one. Stay near a telephone, Tim. I could need you in a hurry," and Dorey hung up.

He pushed back his chair and stared sightlessly across the room, his mind busy.

If this man was really Henry Sherman, he thought, what in the world was he doing in Paris? He was pretty sure that O'Halloran was right and this man was Sherman. Had Sherman gone out of his mind? Dorey dismissed this thought immediately. The fact that Mary Sherman had obviously helped her husband to make this dangerous and mysterious journey must mean that they were both involved in a very serious, personal matter which had forced Sherman to sneak out of the country and come to Paris.

Dorey wiped his damp hands on his handkerchief. If the Press got hold of this story! Henry Sherman of all people, in a disguise and travelling on a false passport!

Dorey had reason to be alarmed for Henry Sherman was running for the Presidency of the United States and so far he was well ahead of the small field. Apart from being the very possible future President, Sherman was one of the richest and most powerful men in America. He was the President of the American Steel Corporation, Chairman of the United American & European Airways, and he held innumerable directorships on various important boards. His influence was considerable and he was on first-name terms with all the important members of the present Government. He had always led an immaculate private life, and his wife, it had been generally agreed, would make the ideal First Lady.

Dorey had known Sherman for some forty-five years. As freshmen, they had shared a room together at Yale University. Thinking back, Dorey realised what a dynamo Sherman had been even at the beginning of his spectacular career and how much Sherman had inspired him to work to gain his own position in the world when there had been times when he could have lagged behind. Dorey was very much aware that it was due to Sherman's influence that he was still at his desk instead of eating his heart out in retirement. He had heard that Sherman had said: "Retire Dorey? Why? Because he is sixty-five? Ridiculous! He has years of experience behind him. He has tremendous drive still and he is utterly ruthless ... we can't afford to be without him ... so keep him!" Dorey remembered this. Although he had to admit that often Sherman was too tough, too anti-Russia, too anti-China and made enemies easily, Dorey felt an unshakeable loyalty towards this man who had done so much for him. If there was anything he could do for Sherman, he wanted to do it. But what should he do in this situation? Sherman was no fool. He must know he was risking his chances of becoming President by coming to Paris as he had done. What a scandal would blow up if this reckless move were to be discovered! The Press of the world would make headlines of it!

Dorey thought for some minutes, then he made his decision. The best thing he could do for Sherman was to do nothing. He knew Sherman was very capable of looking after himself. O'Halloran had been warned to do nothing. Hammer was a good agent and he wouldn't talk. Dorey decided to let Sherman remain anonymous, to do what he had come to do, then return to his supposed sick bed. If no one interfered, Sherman would do exactly this, but suppose someone did? Dorey looked out at the sunshine and at the green trees. The view no longer held any charms for him. Suppose the French police picked Sherman up and charged him with travelling on a false passport? Suppose some crackpot who hated him – as many crackpots hated him – recognised him and assassinated him? Suppose …

Dorey flinched. Anything could happen to a man of Sherman's stature. But what was he to do?

As if in answer to this question, the telephone bell buzzed.

"What is it?" Dorey snapped, anxious not to be disturbed from his line of thinking.

"I have a caller on the line, sir," Mavis Paul said. "He won't give his name. He says you and he were at Yale together."

Dorey drew in a long breath of relief.

"Put him through at once."

There was a brief pause, then a man's voice said, "Is that you, John?"

"Yes. Don't identify yourself. I know who you are. I am entirely at your service. Is there anything I can do?"

"I want to see you … it's urgent."

Dorey cast a quick eye at his engagement diary. He had two appointments set up within the next two hours, but neither of them was important.

"Where are you?"

"Hôtel Parc, Rue Meslay."

"I'll be with you in twenty minutes. Please remain in your room. I take it I ask for Mr Jack Cain?" Dorey couldn't resist this and it pleased him to hear a startled catch of breath at the other end of the line.

"Yes, but ..."

"I'm on my way." Dorey hung up, snatched his coat and hat from the rack and walked quickly into the outer office.

Mavis Paul, dark, beautifully built and very assured, paused in her typing. She had been with Dorey now for a little over a year, and both of them had come to respect each other. Mavis was conscientious, serious, in spite of her glamour, ambitious and a ferocious worker: all qualities that Dorey admired, but at this moment, he was not in an admiring mood.

His cold, set expression startled Mavis.

"I may not be back before three," he said, scarcely pausing. "Cancel my appointments. Say I am not well," and he was gone.

Mavis was too experienced not to put two and two together. O'Halloran had telephoned: a stranger had telephoned, and now her boss had shot off like a rocket. These brief events added up to trouble, but Mavis was used to trouble. She shrugged her pretty shoulders and reached for her address book to cancel the appointments.

Dorey drove his Jaguar to Hôtel Parc, a small, dingy hotel near Place de la République. As was to be expected in this *arrondissement* – as in all *arrondissements* of Paris – he found no parking space. He finally left the Jaguar on a pedestrian crossing within a minute's walk from the hotel, certain a *contravention* would be waiting under his windscreen wiper on his return.

Reaching the hotel, he paused to regard the entrance, thinking at least Sherman had been discreet. No one in their right minds would imagine the future President of the United States would stay at such a place.

He pushed open the glass door, smeared with fingerprints, and entered the tiny lobby that smelt of garlic and faulty drains. A bald-headed, fat man sat behind the reception desk, aimlessly turning the pages of *Le Figaro*. Behind him was a rack of keys and by his side, a small, antiquated telephone switchboard.

"Monsieur Jack Cain?" Dorey said, coming to rest in front of the desk.

The bald-headed man blinked sleepily.

"Who, monsieur?"

Dorey repeated the name.

Reluctantly, the bald-headed man took a tattered register from a drawer and examined it. Then he nodded his head as he said, "Room 66, monsieur. Third floor." He then returned to his aimless reading.

As he climbed the three flights of stairs, covered by green, threadbare carpet, the smells seemed to grow stronger and Dorey wrinkled his nose. He reached the third-floor landing, walked along a dimly lit corridor until he found Room 66. He paused, aware that his heart was beating a little too fast. He wasn't sure if it was because of the climb or because he was about to face the future President of the United States.

He rapped gently on the door. After a brief pause, the door opened.

"Come in, John."

Dorey moved into a small, shabbily furnished bedroom and Henry Sherman closed and locked the door. The two men regarded each other.

Sherman was an imposing, massive figure of a man in his late fifties. Some six feet three inches tall, he had broad shoulders, a fleshy, deeply tanned face, piercing, steel-blue eyes and a thin hard mouth. He was not only handsome, but he exuded that authoritative air and personality that put him in the top echelon of VIPs.

Dorey hadn't seen him now for some five years. He could see the change in him. Something pretty bad must have happened, Dorey decided, for Sherman to look so haggard and to have these black smudges of worry under his steel-blue eyes.

"It's good to see you again, John," Sherman said. "Thank you for coming so quickly." He paused, looking at Dorey, then went on, "How did you get onto Jack Cain?"

Dorey slid out of his coat. As Sherman sat on the bed, Dorey took the only upright chair.

"You were spotted leaving Orly, sir," he said quietly. "Your embarkation card was checked. O'Halloran called me. I told him to lay off."

Sherman passed his hand over his face. His massive shoulders sagged a little.

"But how could I have been spotted?" he asked without looking up.

"Alec Hammer covers Orly. You remember him? He recognised your walk."

Sherman looked up. His tired face split into a rueful grin.

"You have good men working for you, John."

"Yes. When do you plan to leave here, sir?"

"I'm booked out on the next flight in three hours' time. Can you guess why I am here?"

Dorey shook his head.

"No, sir. Something pretty urgent, of course. You're taking one hell of a risk ... but I don't have to tell you that."

Again Sherman smiled wearily.

"I know it, but Mary and Cain co-operated. Otherwise, I would never have got here." He leaned forward, his massive hands on his knees and stared directly at Dorey. "I am here because you are the only man I can rely on to keep me in the Presidential race ... and I mean that."

Dorey shifted uneasily, but his deadpan expression didn't change.

"It will be my pleasure, sir, to do the best I can. What am I to do?"

Sherman continued to stare at him.

"You mean that?"

"Yes ... I mean it."

"I knew I could rely on you, John. Goddamn it! You and I are old friends. When this mess blew up, I told Mary you were the only one I could trust to help. Mary fixed it. Without her, I'd never have got here." There was a pause, then Sherman went on, "I haven't much time. I want you to see something, then we'll talk. Sit where you are."

He got to his feet, crossing the room to where his suitcase stood against the wall. From the suitcase he took an 8 mm film projector, neatly stowed away in its blue carrying case. Quickly, he assembled the machine, threaded on a spool of film, then set the projector on the shabby dressing-table. He plugged into the lamp socket, pulled the thick, dusty curtains, shutting out the late morning sunlight.

Dorey watched all this uneasily.

Neither man said anything until Sherman had switched on the projector, quickly focusing the picture on the grubby white wall in front of Dorey, then he said, "I've seen this. I don't want to see it again." He crossed the room, his body cutting off the picture on the wall for a brief moment, then he sat on the bed, his face in his hands, his eyes staring bleakly at the threadbare carpet by the bed.

Dorey watched the film. It was one of those blue films so popular at American stag parties: obscene, crude, sexually brash and to Dorey utterly disgusting. The male participant had a black hood over his head, disguising his features. The girl was around twenty-two years of age, dark, sun-tanned and sensually and sensationally built. The film lasted some five minutes and Dorey was relieved when the spool ran out. He had often heard of these blue films, but he had never seen one before. He was shocked to see living proof on this film that a man and a woman could behave in a way no animal would behave. He felt a sense of outrage. What was Sherman thinking of, showing him this filth?

As the end of the film began to flick around in its spool, Sherman got up, switched off the projector, then walked across the room and drew back the curtains. He turned and looked at Dorey who had taken off his spectacles and was looking anywhere but at Sherman.

Sherman said quietly, his voice unsteady, "The girl in that film, John, is my daughter."

*   *   *

As Captain O'Halloran was pleased that his agent, Alec Hammer, had been alert enough to identify Henry Sherman so too was Serge Kovski, head of the Paris division of Soviet Security, pleased that his agent, Boris Drina, had also identified Sherman.

Drina, a fat, suety-faced, nondescript-looking man in his late forties, spent much of his time hanging around Orly airport. Kovski had placed him there because he knew Drina lacked courage and brains and was idle. The only reason why Drina was retained as an agent was because he possessed an extraordinary photographic memory. Once he had had a glimpse of someone, he could identify him, even after a long period of time. Imprinted on his mind were this man's characteristics, his features and even the sound of his voice.

Four years ago, Henry Sherman, with his wife, had arrived at Orly for a dinner with the President of France. Drina had seen this tall, massively built man leave Orly, and the camera in Drina's mind had photographed this man's movements, his swinging walk, the quick jerk of his head and the sound of his voice. All this remained an undeveloped negative in Drina's mind until he spotted Sherman, now wearing a moustache and dark glasses move from behind the *Douane* barrier and make his way quickly to the taxi rank.

Drina knew immediately that this man was the likely President of the United States. Unlike Alec Hammer who couldn't believe the evidence of his eyes and hesitated, Drina relied on his photographic memory and immediately moved into action. He followed Sherman, and as Sherman was taking the only taxi on the rank, Drina was close enough to hear him say, "Hôtel Parc, Rue Meslay."

Drina had managed to get this close by pretending to take the taxi while Sherman was speaking to the driver.

Seeing him about to get into the taxi, Sherman said curtly, "This is mine, monsieur."

Drina lifted his shabby hat that looked like a drowned cat and backed away.

"Excuse me."

As soon as the taxi had driven off, Drina walked quickly to the nearest telephone kiosk. Any exertion made him breathless as he lived on a diet of vodka, onion soup and too much bread. Before putting through the call to Kovski, he paused to get back his breath.

His report electrified Kovski. Knowing Drina's reliable, photographic memory, Kovski didn't waste time querying if Drina just might be mistaken.

The two men spoke in Russian.

Kovski said, "Go to the Hôtel Parc immediately. I will send Labrey there. Every move Sherman makes must be reported to me. I will see Labrey has a radio car. Go at once. You have done well."

Drina had his own car parked at Orly. Even while Alec Hammer was still talking to O'Halloran, Drina half-ran, half-walked to his car, then scrambling breathlessly into the car, he started the engine.

You have done well was music to his ears. He couldn't remember when last Kovski had given him any praise. His heart beating fast, his breath wheezing through his fat covered lungs, Drina sent his Renault shooting along the auto route towards Paris.

＊　　　＊　　　＊

The girl in this film is my daughter.

For a moment Dorey again wondered if his hearing was failing, but one look at Sherman's haggard face and the cold misery in his eyes told him he had heard aright.

Dorey's mind worked swiftly. Vaguely now, he remembered hearing that Sherman had a daughter. The last time he had heard anything of her was that she was being educated at an expensive school in Switzerland. When was that? Possibly six or seven years ago. Since then he had heard nothing of her. Whenever Sherman and his wife went on vacation, attended premières or important dinners, the daughter was conspicuous by her absence. Dorey recalled the girl in the film. Now he knew who she was, he realised she took after her mother. She had Mary's beauty, Mary's slimness, long legs and beautiful hands.

"I'm sorry, sir," was all he could say.

"Yes." Sherman sat on the bed. "You'd better hear the whole, sordid story, John." He paused, rubbing his hand across his face. "Gillian and I have never hit it off." He looked directly at Dorey. "I guess it was half my fault ... half hers. Maybe more my fault than hers because I didn't want children. Anyway, from the very beginning when she was a baby, we resented each other and she was a complete little hellion. She deliberately set out to be difficult, making blackmailing scenes, yelling and screaming if she didn't get her own way. When she reached her teens she became insufferable ... anyway to me. How the hell can a man work when there is pop music, longhaired creeps, shouting and yelling, Gillian kicking up trouble every hour of the day? I just couldn't stand it any longer. Why the hell should I? It was my house and Gillian turned it into a goddamn zoo. So I packed her off to Switzerland. The school was top class and they promised to discipline her. She remained in Switzerland, not coming home at all, for four years. God! It was a relief to get her out of my hair ... you have no idea the peace I had once she had gone! Well, she stayed at the school until she was nineteen. By then Mary and I were used to living without her." Sherman looked down at his massive hands, frowning. "Both of us were constantly busy. When we found time to take a vacation we went with a group of people who were helping me build my political career ... there was no place for a teenage daughter. Anyway, Gillian would have been bored stiff with the people I moved around with, so we arranged for her to stay in Europe. We wrote regularly, of course. She didn't seem to be interested in anything so I suggested she should study architecture. She agreed. I found a woman professor to go around with her, teach her, take her to France, Germany and Italy and generally keep an eye on her. Then eighteen months ago, I heard from her professor that she had packed her things and had gone off into the blue." Sherman paused. "I thought maybe this was the best thing that could happen. I was busy ... Mary, of course, was worried, but frankly, John, Mary was also busy ... she wants to become the First Lady as much as I want to become the President."

Dorey was only half-listening to this. He couldn't get out of his mind the pictures of the naked girl he had watched with so much disgust. Sherman's daughter! He felt a chill run up his spine. If this film got into the wrong hands, not only would Sherman be politically finished, but his social life would also be ruined.

Sherman was saying, "Of course I accept some of the blame. We've behaved selfishly, but Gillian just doesn't fit in with our way of life nor we with hers. I thought it best to let her make her own life. I was ready to give her money, but she never asked for it." He paused to stare at Dorey who sat motionless, his legs crossed, his hands in his lap. "We tried to bury her, and this is the result."

"Yes," Dorey said, feeling he was expected to say something. "I understand."

Sherman forced a rueful smile.

"That's because you are loyal to me, John. Most people would say I deserve what I'm getting. We have been neglectful parents and now we are reaping the whirlwind ... and my God! ... what a hell of a whirlwind!" He took from his wallet a piece of paper and handed it to Dorey. "Take a look at this."

Dorey unfolded the paper. The typewritten note ran:

To the Sucker who imagines he is going to be the President.

We send you a souvenir from Paris. We have three other similar souvenirs even better (or worse), than this one. If you continue to run for election, these souvenirs will be sent to your Opposition Party who will know what to do with them.

Dorey studied the uneven typing. He held the letter up to the light, studying the faint watermark.

"You have the envelope, sir?"

"The film and the letter came in the Diplomatic bag," Sherman said. He opened a briefcase, lying on the bed and took out a stout manila envelope. He handed it to Dorey.

The envelope was addressed to:

Mr Henry Sherman,
534, Whiteside Crescent. Washington.
c/o American Embassy. Paris.
Please forward. Personal & Urgent.

There was a pause, then Sherman said, "Well, John? You see why I am here. Someone in Paris – and this is your territory – is blackmailing me to give up running for the Presidency. Mary and I have talked it over. She wanted me to give up, but then I thought of you. Jack Cain has always served me well. I went to see him in hospital, told him I had to come to Paris and asked him to lend me his passport. He gave it to me without hesitation even though he knew if this leaked, he'd lose his job. So, here I am. If you can't come up with a solution, I'll have to withdraw from the election. I don't have to tell you that being the President means more

16

to me than anything that has happened in my life so far. Can you come up with a solution?"

Dorey's agile mind was already busy with the problem. Seeing his expression of concentration, Sherman sat back and lit a cigar with an unsteady hand. He had to wait several minutes before Dorey said, "I could find this blackmailer in a few days and I could put him out of business. I have the men and the organisation to do it. That's why I'm in office. But this isn't the solution, I'm afraid." He looked directly at Sherman. "You and I are friends. We have things in common. You have done a lot for me, and I would more than welcome the opportunity to do something for you. But you have enemies. Some of my men wouldn't want you as President. They don't agree with your views ... that's their privilege. It would be impossible for me to use my network on this problem without one or maybe more of my agents deliberately leaking the news that your daughter is in a blue film. I'm putting this bluntly because we haven't much time. As I see it, I can't use my organisation to help you. You know how my system works. Every assignment I work on has its own file: a copy always goes to Washington. To open a file on this problem is unthinkable. I'm sorry, sir, but that is the position."

Sherman rubbed his hand over his face, then lifted his massive shoulders in a resigned shrug.

"Mary said more or less the same thing. I know you are right, John. I had a faint hope that you might be able to help, but I didn't pin much on that hope." Again he shrugged. "So, okay, I'm caught. At least it was a try."

"I didn't say I can't help you, sir. I said my organisation can't help you," Dorey said quietly.

Sherman looked sharply at him.

"You can help me?"

"I think so. It will cost money."

Sherman made an impatient movement.

"What's money to me? I don't give a damn what it costs. How can you help me?"

"I could offer this assignment to Girland. If anyone can swing it, he can."

"Girland? Who is he?"

Dorey smiled wryly.

"You may well ask. Girland was once one of my top agents, but I had to get rid of him. He was too much the rebel. He always put himself first. He has no social conscience and he moves so close to dishonesty I marvel he isn't in jail. He has swindled me out of considerable sums of money. He is tough, ruthless, an expert Karate fighter and a first-class shot. He is dangerous, calculating, shrewd and tricky. He has a lot of courage and I am not saying this lightly. He has lived for years in Paris. He knows Paris the way I know the back of my hand. He mixes with every kind of crook, conman, swindler, tart and queer. He has shady contacts everywhere. Those who live in the shadows trust him. He has two obsessions: money and women. If there is anyone who can solve your problem, it is Girland."

Sherman looked uneasily at Dorey.

"Are you sure, John? A character like that could also attempt to blackmail me once he knew the set-up. Surely you're not serious?"

"Girland would never blackmail anyone. In his odd way, he has his standard of ethics. I know Girland. He is a rebel and he is tricky, but if he accepts an assignment, I have never known him not to deliver the goods. He is your only hope, sir. I wouldn't say this unless I was sure."

Sherman hesitated, then raised his hands helplessly.

"I have no alternative then, have I? If you really believe we should hire this man and he can fix it, then let's hire him. Will he take the assignment?"

Dorey smiled sourly.

"Give Girland a whiff of money and there is no job he won't do. It'll probably cost you twenty thousand dollars. I'll try to get him for less of course. With that kind of money hanging in front of his nose, Girland would undertake to kidnap Charles de Gaulle."

*   *   *

Drina found Paul Labrey lounging at a table outside a café that faced Hôtel Parc. He sat down heavily beside Labrey, took off his hat and wiped his balding, sweating forehead.

"Anything happened?" he asked.

"Your man arrived fifteen minutes ago," Labrey said, not looking at Drina. "He's in there now."

"Nothing else?"

"No."

Drina continued to mop his face. He scowled at Labrey whom he disliked, knowing Labrey regarded him with contempt and looked on him as a joke.

Paul Labrey was twenty-five years of age. His French mother, now dead, had been a waitress in a lowly bistro. His father, whom he had never known, had been a passing American soldier.

Labrey was tall, painfully thin with thick flaxen hair that reached to his shoulders. His skin was milky-white, his mouth wide and hard and his hazel eyes shifty. Green tinted sunglasses were never off his face. Some of his friends thought he even slept in them. He wore a black turtle neck sweater and black hipsters that seemed to be painted on him. He was known to be dangerous and vicious in a fight.

He was also known to be cunning, quick witted and a Communist.

One of Kovski's agents had come across him in a cellar club, addressing a group of hippies, explaining to them the theory of Communism. The agent was so impressed by what he heard that he alerted Kovski. Labrey had been interviewed and accepted as an agent, and was now drawing enough money from the Russian Security police to live the life he wanted to live, but he, in turn, gave service.

Kovski often found Labrey useful since American tourists were only too happy when Labrey introduced himself and offered to show them the more seamy side of Paris nightlife. The Americans talked to him and he listened and reported back. Kovski often marvelled at the amount of loose talk that went on among VIP American tourists when they came to Paris and had too much to drink and were enjoying themselves. Labrey had a good memory. Much of what he reported was of no interest, but every now and then something would crop up of importance and this was relayed to Moscow. Kovski considered Labrey an excellent investment at eight hundred francs a month.

The barman from the café came out into the sunshine and stood over Drina.

"Monsieur?"

Drina would have liked to have had a vodka, but he was afraid that Labrey would report back that he was drinking spirits while on duty. Sullenly, he ordered a coffee.

As the barman returned to the café, Labrey said, "Why don't you buy yourself a new hat? That thing looks like a drowned dog."

Drina was sensitive about his hat. He couldn't afford to buy a new one, but even if he had had the money, he would not have parted with this hat. It was his one link with his happier days when he lived in Moscow.

"Why don't you have a haircut?" he snarled. "You look like a lesbian!"

Labrey hooted with laughter.

"You improve with age," he said when he stopped laughing. "That's not bad! Maybe you aren't such a dummy as you look."

"Shut up!" Drina said furiously. "Back in Moscow, I would have ..."

But Labrey wasn't listening. He was still chuckling. "Lesbian! I love that! I must tell Vi."

Drina suddenly sat upright as he saw John Dorey walk quickly along the Street, pause for a long moment to survey the dingy Hôtel Parc, then enter.

Labrey looked questioningly at Drina, seeing his face stiffen. "Don't go theatrical on me, comrade ... someone you know?"

"Shut up!" Drina snapped. He went into the café and shut himself into a telephone kiosk. He called Kovski.

"What is it?" Kovski demanded.

"John Dorey has arrived at Hôtel Parc," Drina said in Russian.

"Dorey?"

There was a pause, then Kovski asked, "Is Labrey with you?"

"Yes."

Kovski thought for a long moment. So Dorey was having a secret meeting with Sherman. This could be of vital importance. He mustn't make a mistake.

"I will send two more men to you immediately. Sherman and Dorey must not be lost sight of ... you understand?"

"Yes."

Drina returned to the outside table and sat down. He removed his hat and mopped his forehead.

"The man who went into the hotel is John Dorey, Director of the CIA," he told Labrey. "Comrade Kovski is sending two more men to help us. Sherman and Dorey must not be lost sight of ... it is an order."

Labrey nodded. His flaxen hair danced on his collar.

*　　*　　*

Serge Kovski was a short fat man with a chin beard, an enormous bald dome of a head, ferrety eyes and a thick, blunt nose. He was shabbily dressed in a baggy black suit and there were food stains on his coat lapels for he was a gross eater.

While he was reading through a mass of papers that had come in the Diplomatic bag, his telephone bell rang.

It was Drina again.

"Sherman has left in a taxi for Orly," Drina reported. "Labrey and Alex are following him. I think Sherman is taking the 15.00 hr flight to New York. Labrey will call you as soon as they arrive at the airport. Max and I followed Dorey. He left Hôtel Parc before Sherman did. He was carrying an 8 mm Kodak movie projector. He must have had this from Sherman as he didn't have it when he arrived. He drove in his car to Rue des Suisses. Leaving his car, he entered an apartment block and walked to the top floor." Drina was deliberately holding back on the final denouement. "The top floor of this building, comrade, is occupied by Mark Girland ... the man we have had trouble with before." Kovski's ferrety eyes narrowed as he listened.

"Very well," he said, after a pause. "Max is to follow Dorey when he leaves. You will follow Girland. Be very careful of Girland. He is tricky. Don't let him see you."

"I understand," Drina said and hung up.

Kovski stared down at his desk while he thought, then with a sneering little smile, he pressed a bell button.

A fat, shapeless, elderly woman came in, a notebook and pencil in her hand.

"Send Malik to me," Kovski said curtly, not looking at her. Now that he had lived in Paris for some eight years, he had become used to seeing the young, slim girls moving on the streets and he secretly lusted for them. Elderly, fat women no longer appealed to him.

The woman went away. A few minutes later the door opened and Malik came in.

Before he had disgraced himself and had fallen from favour, Malik was considered to be the most dangerous and the most efficient of all the Soviet agents.

He was a giant of a man; a splendid looking athlete with silver blond hair cut short. His square-shaped face, with its high cheekbones, its powerful, aggressive jaw, its short, blunt nose revealed his Slav extraction. His flat, green eyes were windows revealing a cold and ferocious ruthlessness that made most people flinch from him.

He and Kovski were bitter enemies. Until the moment when Malik had fallen from disgrace, he had always treated Kovski with cold contempt. Although Kovski was his senior in rank, Malik never accepted this fact, and Kovski was too cowardly to attempt to exert his authority over this menacing giant. But now, once the news broke that Malik was no longer considered the best agent and had been removed from the active field and given a desk job, Kovski decided at last he could take revenge on this man who had treated him so contemptuously. He had written to his own superior, suggesting that Malik should be transferred to Paris, pointing out that he could use him usefully as he was behind in his paperwork and Malik could make a trusted clerk. Kovski's boss also hated Malik and he appreciated Kovski's sense of humour. So Malik was sent to Paris and loaded down with routine and dull paperwork. There was nothing he could do about it except continue to hate Kovski and bide his time.

The two men looked at each other.

"I didn't hear you knock," Kovski growled.

Malik inclined his head.

"Because I didn't." He looked around, drew up an upright chair and sat astride it, staring at Kovski with his bleak, snake's eyes.

For a brief moment, Kovski wanted to tell Malik to stand while he was talking to him, but he hadn't the nerve. There was that deadly menace lurking in the green eyes that warned Kovski that Malik could be pushed so far, and no further. He knew Malik had only to reach out and grip his neck in his huge killer's hands for him to die quickly and unpleasantly.

"You have a chance to get back into favour," Kovski said with his sneering smile. "Listen carefully." He told Malik what he had learned about Sherman's arrival, how Dorey had seen Sherman and had left with a movie projector.

"And this should interest you: Dorey is now talking to Girland ... the man who has always defeated you in the field who is responsible for your present disgrace*. I must know what is happening. You are to take over this assignment. Labrey, Drina, Alex and Max are already working on this. You must find out why Dorey has this movie projector: why Sherman has been here: why Girland is being consulted. I want immediate action. Do you hear me?"

Malik stood up.

*see *Have This One On Me*, by James Hadley Chase.

"Deafness is not among my many failings," he said, and without looking at Kovski, he left the room.

2

A little after 10.00 hrs on this bright May morning, Girland came awake. He came awake by slow degrees, groaning a little, stretching and yawning, then remembering he had work to do, he heaved himself reluctantly from under the sheet and walked with eyes half shut into the shower-room. Still only half-awake, he ran his electric shaver over his face, moaning softly to himself and feeling like a resurrected corpse.

He had had an exhausting evening and the girl who had been with him had been young and wildly enthusiastic. He had been glad to see her go, and thankful she hadn't insisted on spending the rest of the night with him.

It wasn't until he had stood under the blast of cold water from the shower for some minutes that he finally came alive, then he discovered he felt fine. He threw on a sweat shirt and a pair of blue hipsters and as he did so, he found he was hungry. He hurried into the kitchenette and peered hopefully into the refrigerator.

A few minutes later two eggs were cooking in a pan of butter and two thick slices of ham were sizzling under the grill. The coffee percolator was performing and Girland now felt much more with the world.

After breakfast, he cleared the table, dumping the used crockery into the sink. Then lighting a cigarette, he placed a mirror from his dressing-table on the table. He found a pack of playing cards, then sitting down in front of the mirror, he began to shuffle the cards.

This evening he had been invited to a poker game. He knew that two of the players were professional card sharpers: the other six were pigeons to be fleeced, and Girland had no intention of being fleeced himself.

He hadn't played serious poker for some time and suspected that his technique might have become rusty. Watching his hands in the mirror, flicking the cards through with lightning speed, he saw that the manoeuvre of bringing all the aces to the top of the deck would be obvious to a trained eye.

He continued to practice for the next hour until he was satisfied that all his rust had been removed. He then began another manoeuvre which was much more difficult: that of dealing himself Ace, King, Queen after eight hands had already been dealt. He was still working on this, the ashtray now overloaded with cigarette butts, when the telephone bell rang.

He put down the cards, hesitated, then shrugging, he crossed the room and picked up the receiver.

"Is that you, Girland?" a voice asked: a voice that sounded oddly familiar.

"If it isn't, some creep is wearing my clothes," Girland returned. "Who is this?"

"I shall be with you in ten minutes ... wait for me," and the line went dead.

Girland replaced the receiver, rubbed the end of his nose and frowned.

"Unless I am very much mistaken," he said aloud, "that sounded very much like that old goat, Dorey."

He looked around the big studio room. It had undergone certain changes for the better since he had lifted several thousand dollars off Dorey. Gone were the canvas deckchairs that had once served him as armchairs. Now the room sported a deep reclining padded chair and a big settee which his girlfriends appreciated very much. There was also a splendid Bukhara rug on the floor: its rich colouring did much to give a tone of luxury to this otherwise dark-looking room.

Humming under his breath, Girland put the mirror back on the dressing-table, emptied his cigarette butts into the trash basket, made his bed and then washed up.

Some fifteen minutes later, he heard footsteps coming up the stairs, then the doorbell rang. He opened the door.

Breathing heavily from the long climb, Dorey surveyed Girland, seeing a slimly-built man, thin-faced with black hair, a few scattered white hairs either side of his temples, dark, alert eyes that often had a jeering light in them, a thin hard mouth and a pronounced almost Wellingtonian nose.

Girland looked at the movie projector Dorey was carrying, then with his jeering smile, he shook his head.

"Not today, thank you ... I never buy anything at the door."

"Don't be impertinent," Dorey said, trying to regain his breath. "I want to talk to you."

With a resigned shrug, Girland stood aside.

"Well, come in. This is a surprise. I thought you had retired long ago and were back in the States with your feet up."

Dorey ignored this. He looked around the room, then eyed the big lush-looking rug, his eyebrows lifting.

"Hmm ... that's a nice rug you have there ... a Bukhara, isn't it?"

"Yes ... thank you very much."

Dorey looked sharply at Girland who was grinning.

"I suppose that means you bought it with the money you stole from me."

Girland laughed.

"Sit down. Take the weight off your feet. It's a long climb for an elderly gentleman ... it even makes me tired sometimes."

Dorey took off his overcoat, dropped it on a chair, then sat down in the big armchair. He surveyed Girland with disapproval.

"I have a job for you."

Girland grimaced, then held out his hands as if to push Dorey away.

"No, thank you. If it is anything like the last job you landed in my lap. I'm not interested. I've finally made up my mind, Dorey, I have had enough of your funny little jobs. I'm getting along very well without you and I intend to continue to get along without you. Working for you is nothing but a pain in the neck."

"This is an unofficial job," Dorey said, crossing one birdlike leg over the other. He suddenly became aware how comfortable the big armchair was. "This is a nice chair you have."

"Glad you like it," Girland said and smiled. "Thank you very much."

Dorey's face suddenly relaxed and he gave his dry, wintry smile.

"You are an amusing rogue, Girland. There are times when I actually find myself liking you. How would you like to pick up ten thousand dollars?"

"Have you been drinking?" Girland lifted his eyebrows. He sat on the settee, then stretched out lengthwise, and eyed Dorey with a shade more interest. "Ten thousand? Not from you ... that would be too much to believe."

"Ten thousand and expenses," Dorey said, sensing that Girland, like a hungry trout, was now beginning to nibble at his bait. "Could be you just might end up with fifteen or even twenty thousand dollars. Does it interest you?"

Girland laced his fingers at the back of his head. He stared up at the ceiling for some moments, then said, "You know something, Dorey? You are not very subtle. You are sure I am for sale. Well, I am not. Every so often you and I get into this kind of huddle and you wave a bait under my nose and I fall for it. So what happens? I pull your chestnuts out of the fire and always land in grief myself. No ... I'll get by without your ten thousand dollars. I'm not interested."

Dorey smiled.

"What's the matter with you, Girland?" he asked. "I thought you still had some guts."

"This kind of talk I love! So now, apart from all this money you're offering, I also have to have guts."

"Let's stop this fooling!" Dorey said, his voice sharpening. "Time is running out. Do you want this job which will pay a guaranteed fifteen thousand dollars or don't you?"

Girland studied Dorey thoughtfully.

"Guaranteed?"

"That's what I said."

"How is this fifteen thousand to be paid?"

"Five thousand tomorrow and ten thousand when the job is done."

Girland shook his head.

"No, Dorey, I don't go along with that, but I might if you paid ten thousand tomorrow and ten thousand when the job is done. Yes ... I just might be tempted on those terms."

Dorey snorted and got to his feet.

"You've heard my terms. I can get anyone to do this job, Girland. Don't imagine you are the only man ..."

"Save it," Girland said and closed his eyes. "Nice to see you looking so well considering your age. Thanks for coming. Goodbye."

Dorey hesitated, then sat down again.

"One of these days, Girland, I'm going to fix you and fix you good. It's time you spent a few years in jail ..."

"Are you still here?" Girland opened his eyes. "The trouble with you, Dorey, is you take life too seriously. It's fatal. Okay, stop looking like an outraged crocodile ... have we a deal or haven't we?"

Dorey choked back his wrath. This was too important to waste further time haggling. Sherman had all the money in the world. He would be furious if he got to know that Dorey was quibbling about money, but it stuck in Dorey's throat to give this insolent layabout such a sum.

"Yes ... we have a deal," he said finally.

Girland eyed him.

"Ten thousand tomorrow morning, and ten thousand when I have fixed this job?"

Dorey drew in an exasperated breath.

"Yes."

Girland swung his legs off the settee and sat up. His face was alert now and his eyes bright.

"Come on ... tell me. Just what is this job?"

Dorey picked up the movie projector.

"Do you understand how to work this? I don't. I want you to see a film."

"Oh, sure." Girland got to his feet, set up the projector, wound on the film and then pulled the long, gold-coloured curtains over the big studio window.

"Nice, aren't they?" he said, fingering the material. "Again, thanks."

"Get on with it!" Dorey snapped. "I can take just so much from you, Girland, but I warn you ..."

"Dorey! That's temper!"

"Look at this film and stop behaving like a delinquent!"

Girland laughed. He switched on the projector, throwing the picture on his white wall. He flopped back on the settee and watched what went on on the film.

When he realised the kind of film he was looking at, he muttered, "Dorey! You surprise me!" Then he said nothing further, but sat forward, his elbows resting on his knees, watching the girl and the hooded man in their shameless act.

Finally the film ran off the spool. Girland got up, turned off the projector and pulled back the curtains.

He returned to the settee and lay on it.

"Go ahead and talk. I don't imagine you brought this thing along for me to see for fun. What's it all about?"

"There are three other films like this," Dorey said. "I must find them. I also want to find the girl in the film. That's the job, Girland. Do you think you can trace these films and find the girl? Try to be honest with me. The films were taken in Paris so I presume the girl is here too. How about it?"

Girland rubbed his hands on his knees as he studied Dorey.

"What's the rest of it?"

"That's as much as you need know," Dorey snapped. "You will be paid ..."

"Oh, cut it out! If I handle this, I want the whole photo. Why are you mixed up in this?"

"That's not your business, Girland. I want you to trace these other three films and find the girl ... that's what you're being paid for."

Girland got up, took a cigarette from a pack on the table and lit it.

"How's our future President keeping these days, Dorey? Is he free from trouble and worries ... is he happy?"

Dorey started as if he had been stung.

"What are you talking about?" he demanded. "What has ...?"

"Come off your ladder!" Girland said impatiently. He returned to the settee and sat down, facing Dorey, his eyes probing and hard. "You forget I get around in this City. You forget I was once one of your dreary agents. You forget I meet and see lots of people you have never heard of. That girl on the film is Gillian Sherman, the daughter of the possible future President of the United States ... God help them! No wonder you've come here offering me all this money. Well, Dorey, for perhaps the first time in your life, you have done the right thing, coming to me. This job is right up my cul-de-sac. Now don't look like a turkey with colic. She's Sherman's daughter, isn't she?"

Dorey drew in a long, slow breath.

"Do you know her?"

"I've seen her ... I don't know her. I ran into her at a pot party. She was stoned. Some little wasp whispered in my ear that she was Sherman's daughter. This would be three months ago ... probably more."

"Do you know where to find her?"

"That's not answering my question. She is Sherman's daughter, isn't she?"

"Yes." Dorey hesitated, then plunged on, "Sherman is being blackmailed. He's been warned to stop running for the Presidency or three more films will be mailed to the Opposition Party. They will not only wash him up as President, but they will utterly ruin him. He came to me for unofficial help. I come to you."

Girland thought for a long moment, his face expressionless.

"It takes some time to dig the facts out of you, doesn't it?" he said finally. "So for twenty thousand dollars, Sherman hopes to become President of the United States with me doing his dirty work."

"Isn't it enough?" Dorey asked, looking anxious.

"Oh yes, but I'm wondering if I want to help him. I don't like him. I may be out of your racket now but I listen and hear things. I know he tried to get rid of his daughter. I don't dig for that. He is a creep who yearns for power and anyone who gets in his way, goes down the hole. I don't like his politics. I wouldn't vote for him. I wouldn't tell him the time if he asked me."

Dorey said quietly, "Would you put the projector in its case for me? I see I am wasting my time with you, Girland."

As he got to his feet, Girland said, "Don't be so touchy. You know I'll do the job. You know if the money is big enough, I'll do any job. You get off. Leave the film with me. I'll let you know something in a day or so."

Dorey regarded him.

"It's a deal then?"

"Oh, sure." Girland sounded bored. "I'm always a sucker for money." He suddenly grinned. "I want ten thousand dollars in traveller's cheques right here tomorrow morning. I'll trust you to pay the balance when the job is done."

"I'll arrange it." Dorey put on his overcoat. "I don't have to remind you to be careful ... if there is the slightest leak..."

"On your way." Girland waved to the door. "This is my pigeon now. You don't have to remind me about anything."

*   *   *

Max Lintz was tall and bony. He had recently come from East Berlin to work for the Soviet Security in Paris. Nearing fifty years of age, balding with deep-set eyes and a thin, sour mouth, he was known to be an expert tracker of men and an expert pistol shot.

Drina liked him. They were of the same age and they got along well together. Whereas Paul Labrey, because of his youth and his manner, often made Drina boil with fury, Lintz had a soothing effect on him.

They were sitting at a café near Girland's apartment, waiting.

"Would you prefer to follow Dorey?" Lintz asked suddenly. I will take care of Girland ... if you wish."

Drina shifted, frowning. This remark implied that he wasn't capable of following Girland and he looked sharply at Lintz.

"We obey orders, comrade. I am to watch Girland. Comrade Kovski said so."

Lintz shrugged.

"As you will, but be careful. Girland is a professional."

Again Drina shifted in his chair.

"So am I." He stared suspiciously at Lintz. "Don't you think so?"

Although Lintz liked Drina, he secretly thought he was well past his prime. He thought Kovski had made a mistake using Drina to watch a man like Girland, but that was Kovski's business.

"Of course," he said.

There was a long pause. Drina sipped his cooling coffee and stared at the entrance to Girland's apartment block.

"I hear Malik is in Paris," Lintz said, "and in disgrace."

"Yes." Drina's little eyes surveyed the café's terrace. There was no one within hearing distance. "A wonderful man, the best."

"Yes. It can happen to any of us."

"Girland tricked him."

"So I heard. How long do you think Malik will remain out of the field?"

Drina hesitated. Again he assured himself no one was listening.

"Kovski hates him."

"Of the two men," Lintz said softly, "I prefer Malik."

This was too dangerous, Drina thought. He merely shrugged his fat shoulders. He loathed Kovski and was terrified of him.

Kovski, to his thinking, was the jackal to Malik's lion.

"Perhaps we had better not discuss this, Max," he said uneasily. "Nothing good ever comes of discussing personalities."

"That's true."

The two men remained sitting on the terrace in silence until they saw Dorey appear and walk towards his parked Jaguar.

"There's my man," Lintz said. "I leave you to pay the bill. Good luck ... and be careful." He got to his feet and crossed to where he had left his shabby Renault 4, climbed in and drove after the Jaguar.

Drina watched him disappear, then putting three francs on the table, he lit a Gauloise and continued his wait. He was nervous. Lintz was right. Girland was a professional. He would have liked Lintz to have taken care of Girland, but his pride wouldn't allow it. Now, thinking that in a little while, he would have to follow this man wherever he went and remain out of sight brought him out into a cold sweat. Suppose he lost him? Suppose Girland spotted him? He licked his dry lips, trying to assure himself that for the past fifteen years he had followed suspects and had always been successful.

He was so unnerved he could no longer sit at the table. He got up, waved to the waiter, indicating he had left payment and walked across the narrow street to where he had parked his Deux Chevaux. He got in and waited.

Ten minutes later, he saw Girland come from his apartment block and saunter down the street. Girland was wearing a short leather coat over his sweater and hipsters. He was smoking, his hand thrust into his coat pocket.

Drina started his car. He watched Girland cross the road and tuck himself into a shabby, beaten-up Fiat 600. Drina followed the Fiat into the mass of traffic, struggling along Rue Raymond Losserand and finally into Avenue du Maine. Here, Girland turned left. Allowing two cars to be between Girland and himself, Drina kept after the Fiat. At Rue de Vaugirard, Girland turned right and drove a few metres down the traffic-packed road before edging his car into a courtyard.

Forced to continue on down the street by the traffic behind him, Drina had just time to see Girland get out of his car before he lost sight of him. Cursing, he drove on, turned off into a side street and was lucky to find a car pulling away from the kerb. He edged the Deux Chevaux into the space. Snapping off the engine and without waiting to lock the car door, he ran back to the courtyard.

The Fiat was still there, but Girland had disappeared. Drina looked around. There were several doorways leading into the courtyard building that stood in a half square. A brass plate on one of the doors caught his eye.

BENNY SLADE
Photographic Studio

Remembering the movie projector, Drina decided that Girland was paying Benny Slade a visit. He now wished Lintz had taken this assignment. When Girland eventually came out of this building, he would drive away. Drina would have to run down the street, get in his car, and by the time he had got back to Rue de Vaugirard, he would have lost Girland. He hesitated for a long moment, then decided he had to have help.

He walked to the entrance of the courtyard, spotted a café further up the road and ran to it.

A few minutes later, he was once more talking to Kovski.

* * *

Unaware that he was being followed, Girland climbed the three flights of stairs to Benny Slade's studio. He leaned on the bell push and waited.

He had known Benny Slade for some years. Benny was an enormously fat, jovial homosexual with a brilliant flair for photography. He ran a very special and lucrative business supplying the luxury hotels where the Americans were to be found with coloured slides and 8 mm colour films of The Girls of Paris. There was nothing pornographic about his work: every shot was artistic, but somehow managed to be titillating. His slides and films had a very brisk sale. Most of the American tourists bought them to show their neighbours back home just what they were missing.

Benny was onto a good thing and he knew it. He kept clear of any smut. He was the *Playboy* of Paris, and he prospered.

The door was opened by a fair, beautiful looking youth clad in skin-tight trousers and a white shirt worn outside the trousers. He gave Girland a coy little smile and lifted carefully plucked eyebrows as he asked, "Yes, monsieur?"

"Is Benny hatching an egg?" Girland asked.

The eyebrows went up and then down.

"Mr Slade is shooting."

"When isn't he? Okay, I'll wait." Girland moved forward, driving the youth into a long corridor lit by rose-pink lamps held in golden hands fixed to the wall. Everything about Benny's studio was artistic. Girland thought it was terrible.

The youth shut the door.

"Who shall I say, monsieur?"

"Girland ... he knows me."

The youth led the way down the corridor and opened a door.

"Will you wait in here, please, monsieur?"

Girland walked into a glossily furnished room with chairs along the walls, a table in the centre littered with the latest magazines, several of Benny's masterpieces of nude girls enormously blown-up, hanging in gilt frames on the wall.

As the youth closed the door, Girland became aware of a girl sitting on a chair in the far corner of the room, a

39

cigarette in her slim fingers, leafing through a copy of *Elle*.

She glanced up and looked Girland over as he was looking her over. Quite a doll, he thought.

The girl was possibly twenty-three or four years of age. She had long silky blonde hair that reached below her shoulders and concealed most of her face. Her eyes were large and the colour of first grade sapphires. Her mouth was made for kissing. Girland eyed her legs: long and slim, the way he liked them. She was wearing a white silk wrap that hung open revealing the swell of her breasts. She seemed to be wearing nothing under the wrap although Girland couldn't be sure about this. She pulled the wrap close to her when she saw Girland was staring.

He gave her his most charming smile.

"Like waiting at the dentist, isn't it? Are you modelling for Benny?"

"That's right." He could see by the sudden interest in her eyes that he appealed to her. "Are you?"

"Me?" Girland laughed and sat down two chairs away from her. "Benny wouldn't want to shoot me. I'm just paying a social call. I'm Mark Girland."

"I'm Vi Martin."

Again they regarded each other. This was a girl, Girland told himself, who could be exciting in bed.

"Do you do much work for Benny?" he asked.

She grimaced.

"About once a month. The competition is fierce. Every little cow with good legs and tits comes rushing here. They'll even be shot for nothing."

"That's tough. What else do you do beside work for Benny?"

"Oh, I model clothes." She was vague enough for Girland to guess this wasn't strictly the truth. "What do you do?"

"I live off the fat of the land," Girland said airily. "I don't believe in work. It's against my principles."

"It's against mine too, but I have to eat."

"A doll with your looks shouldn't have to worry."

She smiled.

"I didn't say I worried. Do you mean you don't do any work?"

"Not if I can avoid it."

"And you live off the fat of the land?" She let the wrap slip a little and Girland had a glimpse of firm, well-rounded thighs before the wrap was whipped into place.

"I get by. Perhaps one of these evenings we could get together over a dinner and I'll tell you about it ... that is if you are interested."

She regarded him, then nodded.

"I could be. I've always wanted to live off the fat of the land and not do any work."

"This sounds as if we have a lot in common. Do you know Chez Garin restaurant?"

Her sapphire coloured eyes opened wide.

"I've heard of it ... isn't it terribly expensive?"

Girland shrugged.

"So-so. The food's good. Perhaps you would like to have dinner with me tonight at nine? We could meet there."

She stared at him, then her face hardened.

"I hate being kidded so you can skip the routine."

"Listen, chérie, I don't kid beautiful dolls," Girland said quietly. "When I invite a doll like you to dinner, she stays invited."

"A girl can get stood up," Vi said bitterly. "I'd look wet, wouldn't I, if I turned up at that restaurant, and you weren't there to take care of the cheque."

"Okay ... if you're that suspicious ... I'll pick you up. Where do you live, unbeliever?"

She relaxed and laughed.

"I'll believe you. Nine o'clock then at Chez Garin." She leaned back in her chair, her eyes sparkling. "Do you have abstract paintings to show me after dinner?"

"Nothing like that," Girland said, meeting her look. "But I do have a beautiful Bukhara rug."

"I've never been asked to do it on the floor before."

"You haven't? It's the rage this season. You don't know what you're missing."

The door burst open and what appeared to be an elephant stamped into the room. This was Benny Slade's normal entrance. In spite of his 280 pounds, he moved always with a quick rushing charge, surprisingly light on his small feet.

Before Girland could avoid the rush, he was engulfed in enormous fat arms and hugged to breasts that felt like plastic balloons, beaten on the back with hands that felt like pads of dough, then pushed back while Benny beamed on him, his enormous, jovial fat face joyful and delighted.

"Mark, my duckie darling! I'm so pleased! Imagine coming here! Only last night, I was dreaming of you and now ... here you are!"

"Throttle back, Benny," Girland said, escaping from the embrace. "You're giving me a bad reputation. We have a lady present."

Benny giggled.

"So like you, pussy-cat." He beamed at Vi. "Hello, baby. This is my very good, nice boyfriend, Mark Girland. He's quite the loveliest man! He ..."

"Benny! Wrap it up!" Girland said sharply. "We've already met. We know each other. Don't be so goddamn exuberant."

Benny's fat face fell.

"Have I said anything wrong?"

"Not yet ... but you are showing signs. Miss Martin is waiting to be shot."

Benny made a motion of dramatic despair.

"Not now, sweetie," he said, turning to Vi. "I'm sorry ... I'm devastated, but I must talk to Mark. You see Alec. Tell him to arrange everything. You know ... he'll give you you-know-what. Then come back the same time tomorrow, huh? I must talk to Mark."

Vi's expression could have frozen an ice cube.

"You mean that little rat will pay me for just sitting here?" she demanded, getting to her feet. "I bet he won't."

"Now, lovie, don't talk that way. You know Alec loves you as I love you."

"Like a mongoose loves a snake."

Benny spluttered into giggles.

"What a darling! Now, listen, lovie, I'll talk to Alec. You pop your clothes on and I'll see Alec pays you." He wrapped a fat arm around Girland's shoulders and led him to the door.

Girland looked back at Vi who smiled at him.

"Operation Bukhara at nine o'clock," he said.

She nodded as Benny half-led, half-dragged Girland out into the corridor.

"Mark! You're not planning to do anything naughty with that girl, are you?" Benny asked as he propelled Girland by sheer weight down the corridor.

"Why not?"

43

"She has a bad boyfriend." Benny led Girland into his private office. "He sticks knives into people."

"So do I."

Girland paused to absorb the room which made him blink.

Benny had lavished a lot of care and money in making this room something very special. The big desk had a top of gleaming copper. The lounging chairs were covered in zebra skins. Ornate orchids, growing behind glass made up the walls. The lighting bathed this big movie set of a room in soft pink.

"Phew!" Girland exclaimed, looking around. "You're doing yourself well, aren't you?"

"Do you like it?" Benny gave a laugh that sounded like a child with whooping cough. "It took me weeks, darling ... honestly. It nearly drove me out of my little mind. But do you really and honestly like it?"

"I think it stinks," Girland said, sinking into a zebra-covered chair.

"Do you ... do you really? I am so glad. I think it does too, but how it throws my clients! They just pee in their pants when they come in here."

"Look, Benny, I'm in a hurry. I want your help."

Benny's face lost its foolish animation. His eyes became alert. He no longer looked soft and stupid.

"My help? Well, of course. Anything for you, sweetheart."

Some months ago, Girland had fixed a blackmailer who was putting the bite on Benny. He had to get very tough with the boy, but he finally fixed him. Had he not succeeded, Benny would have been out of business: the bite had been a big one. From that moment, Benny was Girland's slave.

"I'll do anything for you, baby," Benny went on. "Ask and you will receive."

"I want you to look at a film. I'm hoping you will know who shot it, where it was shot and who the man is in the film. This is blackmail again, and urgent."

"Let me see it. Come into the studio."

"This is Top Secret, Benny. I wouldn't show you this film if I wasn't sure you won't talk about it."

"That's okay, sweetie. I once relied on you. You can rely on me."

His fat face serious now, Benny led the way into the big studio with its screens, lights, photographic equipment and a king-sized bed mounted on a golden dais on which most of the girls were photographed.

The blond youth who had let Girland in was busy loading film into a camera.

"Run along, Alec, my pet," Benny said. "Give Vi some money. She's dressing."

"But she hasn't done any work," Alec said scowling.

"Never mind ... we must never be mean ... just give her something. She'll be back tomorrow."

Alec shrugged and left the studio. Benny shot the bolt on the door.

"We're quite alone now," he said. "Let's see the film."

This was not strictly accurate for Vi Martin had come quietly into the studio to collect her handbag. Alec hadn't seen her, and hearing Benny and Girland coming down the passage, she had stepped behind one of the big screens. Girland intrigued her. She was curious to know what his business was with Benny.

Girland handed over the 8 mm film. Benny threaded it onto a projector. He cut the lights and threw the picture on a beaded screen.

The two men stood side-by-side watching the film. Vi took a chance and peered out from behind her screen. She had only a brief glimpse of what was going on in the film before she ducked back again.

When the film was finished and Benny had put on the lights, he said, "Who's the girl? I know most of them who work in this racket, but she's new to me."

"Never mind about her." Girland sat on a nearby table and swung his legs. "She doesn't interest me. Any idea who shot the film?"

Benny scratched his ear as he thought.

"There are six boys in Paris making these films." He perched himself on a stool and regarded Girland. "There's big money in this racket, but it's dicey. You never know when you're going to get the flicks on your collar, but these boys are ready to take chances so long as they collect. Now take that film we've just seen. At a rough guess, it's worth thirty thousand dollars. The way this racket works is these boys make the film, run off copies, smuggle them into England and America where they sell around a hundred dollars a spool ... sometimes more. We have a big market here, of course. Each boy has his own particular camera technique. I would say Pierre Rosnold shot that film. I can't swear to it, but the lighting and the camera angles have Rosnold's touch."

"Where do I find him?"

"He has a studio on Rue Garibaldi. His front cover is high-class studio portraits for movie stars and society people ... you know the drag, but his folding money comes from blue films."

"Do you know him?"

Benny's fat face wrinkled in disgust.

"I wouldn't be seen with him in the same toilet. I loathe the beast."

"And the man in the film?"

"That's a problem with that hood. Rosnold has a permanent stallion for these movies: Jack Dodge ... he's an American. I've never met him, but I hear he always wears a hood on these films because he doesn't want to be recognised. He works at Sammy's Bar where simply hordes of ghastly American tourists go." Benny shifted his enormous buttocks on the stool. "The girl interests me. She's an amateur of course, but she has great technique. She could be making herself nice money ... and I mean nice."

"I'm not interested in her," Girland said. "There are three other films, Benny. I've got to find them. It looks as if I'll have to call on Rosnold and twist his arm a little."

Benny's small eyes widened.

"Be careful, darling. He's a toughie."

Girland slid off the table.

"So am I." He grinned at Benny. "Well, thanks. I'll go talk to Rosnold."

Benny rewound the film and gave it to Girland.

"Anything else I can do, give me a call."

They walked together to the door and Benny slid back the bolt.

As they moved out into the corridor, Vi Martin came from behind the screen. She ran silently across the studio to the dressing-room and began hurriedly to dress.

*   *   *

With sweat running down his face, Drina kept looking at his watch. Kovski had promised to rush a man down to where he was waiting, but up to now the man hadn't arrived.

What was he to do if the man didn't arrive and Girland appeared and drove off in his car? He would be held responsible for losing Girland! He knew Kovski was already displeased with his work. He could get into serious trouble.

He took off his shabby hat and wiped the sweat off his balding head. He moved from one foot to the other. His heart hammered and his mouth was dry.

Then he saw Girland come out of the building.

Drina was unprepared. He shouldn't have been standing in the entrance to the courtyard. He should have concealed himself in one of the many doorways leading into the big apartment block. It was too late now. He lost his head and turned quickly, walking into the street. Had he not moved so quickly, Girland wouldn't have noticed him, but that panicky movement alerted Girland. He saw the short, fat man wearing a greasy fur hat dart into the street and Girland's eyes narrowed.

He had decided, as he had descended the stairs from Benny's studio, that as Rosnold's studio was close by, he would walk rather than chance finding parking space. So he sauntered out of the courtyard and almost cannoned into Drina who wasn't sure whether to dart to the right or left.

The two men looked at each other.

Girland too had a photographic memory. He placed Drina immediately: a washed-up, hack Soviet agent of the Security police.

"Pardon," Girland said, moved around Drina and set off with his long strides towards Boulevard Pasteur.

Hardly believing his luck, Drina went after him. He had to half-run to keep up with Girland's swinging strides and sweat ran down his face as he bounced along, dodging people on the sidewalk, but keeping Girland in sight.

Girland was thinking: is this a coincidence? I don't think so. Have the Russians got onto Sherman?

He reached Boulevard Pasteur and stopped at a busy Bistro. It was lunchtime and he decided to have lunch. He entered the Bistro and took a vacant table at the far end of the big room.

Drina saw him enter the Bistro and hesitated. He too was hungry. He again hesitated, then sat at one of the outside tables where he could watch the exit.

From his table, Girland could see the outside terrace and he watched Drina take a seat at a table.

When the waiter came, Girland ordered a steak and a lager. Drina, outside, ordered a ham roll and a vodka.

Drina had placed himself in a bad position. He could watch the exit from the Bistro, but he couldn't see Girland. Aware of this, Girland got to his feet and went to a telephone kiosk. He called Dorey.

When the connection was made, Girland said, "I think our Soviet friends have become interested in our movie. I have Drina on my tail."

Dorey knew Drina as he knew every Soviet agent operating in Paris.

"You have the film on you?"

"Of course."

"Where are you?"

Girland told him.

"I'll send two men down to cover you. Stay where you are."

"Hitch up your suspenders!" Girland said impatiently. "I can handle this. Wake up! You can't send two of your jerks down here to cover me unless you make this official."

Dorey swallowed this, knowing Girland was right.

"But if they jump you and get that film ...!"

"They won't get it. Stop laying an egg! I'll lose this fat slob and I'll call you later. I just thought I'd increase your blood pressure," and Girland hung up.

When he returned to his table, his steak was placed before him. It looked very good. He made a leisurely lunch, paid the bill, then wandered out onto the busy boulevard.

Drina gave him a few metres start, then went after him. Girland wandered along, taking his time. Satisfied now that Girland hadn't spotted him, Drina loafed along in the rear.

Girland was an expert at losing a tail. When he came upon a crowd of people staring at a TV programme showing in a radio shop window, he stepped around them swiftly and into a doorway. The movement was so quick Drina didn't see it. Suddenly Girland had vanished. Drina paused, people pushing by him. In a panic, Drina rushed past the doorway in which Girland was standing to the crossroads. He looked frantically to right and left.

Watching the panic-stricken face of the fat agent, Girland grinned.

3

On the top floors of most of the older apartment blocks in Paris there are a number of small rooms known as *Chambre de bonne* where servants who worked for the owners of the apartments below used to live. But now servants were almost impossible to find, the owners rented these miserable little rooms to students or to those unable to afford higher rents.

Vi Martin lived in one of these rooms on the eighth floor of an old-fashioned block in Rue Singer. The room was equipped with a toilet basin, a portable electric grill, a bed, one small battered armchair and a plastic wardrobe. There was a table under the attic window on which stood a small transistor radio that never ceased to churn out swing music from the moment Vi woke to the moment she went to sleep. She just could not imagine anyone not living in the perpetual din of swing music.

There were eight other little rooms on her floor. Four of them were occupied by elderly women who went out early every day on cleaning jobs. There were two Spanish couples who worked as servants in the apartments below and two elderly widowers who worked at the post office, a few doors down the street.

These people had the habit of leaving their doors open so they could converse with their neighbours without leaving their rooms.

These conversations were carried on at the top of their voices so the din, plus Vi's transistor, was a nightmare bedlam of noise.

Vi shared her room with Paul Labrey. They had met at a Left Bank party and Vi had immediately fallen for Labrey. She thought he was terribly with it with his green tinted glasses and his long hair. He told her as they were dancing that he was sharing a room with a Senegalese who was planning to get married and he would have to move out. Did she know of a cheap room he could rent? Under the influence of six large gins and feeling sexually aroused by the way he was holding her, Vi suggested he should move into her pad and share the rent.

Labrey's hands moved down her back as he regarded her. He decided he could do a lot worse and moved in the following day, bringing with him an old battered suitcase and a few tattered paperbacks.

When Vi asked him what he did for a living, he grinned. "I sell dirty postcards on Place de la Madeleine. It's a good racket. I catch the tourists when they leave Cook's."

She didn't believe this, for often he wouldn't return to the room until well after 03.00 hrs and sometimes he would rush off, swearing, before 08.00 hrs. She was sure he did some shady work – probably in drugs – but she didn't care. Vi was that kind of a girl. At least he always seemed to have a reasonable amount of money and wasn't mean with it. After a little persuasion, and after living with her for two months, he even agreed to pay the whole of the rent, and when they ate out at the bistro in Rue Lekain, he always picked up the tab.

She enjoyed sleeping with him in the single bed. He had a lot of technique and wasn't selfish in his lovemaking. He was fairly easy to live with. There were times when he revealed a quick, dangerous temper, and once when she nagged him about his dirty fingernails, he slapped her bare bottom so viciously, her screams brought their neighbours tapping on their door. That taught Vi, as nothing else could, not to nag.

Until she was seventeen, Vi lived with her parents in Lyons. Her father was well off and retired. Vi had always been a rebel. She loathed the provincial life in Lyons. She dreamed of Paris. Finally, she persuaded her father to let her study English at the Sorbonne. She learned without regret that both her parents had been killed in a car crash. She inherited three hundred thousand francs. She promptly gave up her studies, hooked up with an American newspaperman, and between the two of them, they ran through the money in two years. The American faded and Vi found herself high and dry with no money. She spent the next two years studying the ceilings of sordid hotel bedrooms while any man with money grunted on top of her.

It was pure luck that she ran across Benny Slade. He was searching for a blonde, long-haired beauty with good legs to work in his studio. Seeing Vi as she walked down Avenue des Champs Elysées looking for a client, he decided she was just what he was looking for.

He put her under contract and paid her a thousand francs a month which covered her rent and food bills.

Vi had no difficulty in dressing herself. When she was short of money she either visited one of the big stores and stole what she needed or found an American tourist who paid her well for her favours. When Labrey appeared on her horizon, she became so much better off, since he paid the rent, that she dropped her street-walking, but remained a nimble shoplifter.

Returning to her room this evening, her mind was full of Girland. Chez Garin! she thought as she dumped her handbag and coat on the bed. Had she a decent dress? She went to the plastic wardrobe and flicked through the dresses hanging there. She decided the Swiss silk red dress she had stolen from Aux Trois Quartiers store only last week would do. She checked on her store of stockings – also stolen, and then examined her collection of shoes. Satisfied that she had the right clothes, she turned on the radio and stretched out on the bed.

She closed her eyes and thought of Girland. What a man! There was something about him that Paul just hadn't got. Paul was tough, young, good-looking, and dangerous, but there was no polish to him. Sometimes she got bored with his green tinted glasses and his long hair. If he would only wash his hair more often perhaps he would look more attractive.

Thinking of his hair, made her think of her own. She scrambled off the bed and regarded herself in the mirror over the washbasin. Her long blonde hair didn't look all that hot, she decided, and she began to fill the basin with hot water.

It was while she was bending over the basin, clad only in white panties and bra, her hair floating in the hot water, Labrey came in.

"If you touch me, I'll throw water over you," Vi said hastily, aware that her position was a strong temptation for his heavy hand.

But Labrey wasn't in the mood for fun and games. His face was sullen as he sat on the bed. The trip out to Orly had been a drag. Seeing Henry Sherman pass through the police barrier, he had assumed that he would board the New York flight. But when he telephoned Kovski and had reported, Kovski had flown into a rage. He wanted to know if Labrey was sure that Sherman had taken that flight.

Impatiently, Labrey had pointed out that he couldn't pass the police barrier himself, so how the hell could he really be sure? Kovski had called him an incompetent, idle idiot and had slammed down the receiver. This criticism infuriated Labrey who could never take any form of criticism.

"What are you doing back at this time – I thought you were working," he said as Vi wrung her hair out over the basin.

"Benny had an unexpected visitor," she explained, wrapping her hair in a towel and making herself a turban. "What a dream of a man! He's taking me out tonight."

Labrey wasn't interested. They had an agreement that when either of them felt like a change of sex partners they need not consult each other.

"You're not bringing him back here!" he snapped. "I'll probably be in."

"Bring him to this hole?" Vi laughed. "As if I would! He has class! We're going to Chez Garin … bet you've never even heard of it."

"I haven't and couldn't care less." Labrey lit a cigarette and let smoke drift down his narrow nostrils. He felt a pang of jealousy. Girls got taken to the top places if they were willing to lie on their backs, he thought bitterly. "You watch it. Any pal of Benny's is a suspect."

"Not this one! He's a real doll! After dinner, he is going to show me his Bukhara rug." Vi giggled excitedly as she began to dry her hair. "He has money. I could have myself a ball for a change."

"What's he doing mixing with a slob like Benny then?" Labrey asked, now a little curious.

"He showed Benny a film ... a stag film. He wanted to know who shot it and who the man in the film was ... don't ask me why."

Behind the tinted glasses, Labrey's eyes became alert.

"Did you get this guy's name?"

"Why, of course! I told you he's taking me out tonight." Vi looked indignant. "You don't imagine I'd go out with a man without knowing his name?"

Labrey sneered.

"No, you wouldn't go out with him, but you would sleep with him. What's his name?"

"Mark Girland if it's any of your business!"

Labrey stiffened. He sat motionless, his brain racing. Drina had often talked of an ex-CIA agent named Mark Girland. "One of Dorey's top men, but they fell out," Drina had said. "A good thing for us. Girland was a nuisance. You should hear what Malik thinks of him!"

Once when Drina and Labrey were together on a job, Girland had passed them, and Drina had pointed him out to Labrey who had stared at the tall, dark man, envying him because he was now out of this rat race of a racket.

"Have you swallowed a wasp or something?" Vi asked, staring at Labrey.

"Is he tall, dark with a big nose?"

"I wouldn't call it big ... it's a dreamy nose."

"Is he tall and dark?" Labrey restrained his impatience with an effort.

"Yes, and handsome."

Labrey had telephoned Drina before signing off. Drina had told him that Girland was now involved somehow with Sherman. Labrey felt a wave of excitement run through him.

"Sit down," he said, patting the bed.

"I'm busy, dopey … can't you see?" Vi turned to the mirror. "I can hear what you say without sitting … ouch!"

Labrey's hand cracked across her buttocks, making a pistol-like report.

"Ooooh! You beast!" Vi cried, dancing with the sting and rubbing herself. She started towards the basin of water when Labrey snarled, "Come here and sit down or you'll get a hiding!"

The note in his voice brought her to an abrupt standstill. She looked at him. His thin, white face had that savage expression she didn't often see, but when she did, it scared her.

"All right, all right, you needn't have hit that hard." She came hurriedly and sat by his side. "What is it? God! You hurt me!"

"I want to know exactly what happened between Girland and Benny. I want every detail … right from the beginning."

"What on earth for?" Vi demanded, bewildered, her eyes opening wide.

Labrey's hand came down on her naked thigh with another vicious slap that made her squeal.

"Talk!"

Hurt and now really scared, Vi talked. At the end of her recital, Labrey said, "You're definitely meeting him at this restaurant at nine o'clock tonight?"

"Yes." Vi rubbed the red mark on her thigh. "Look what you've done to me, you stinking brute!"

"Shut up!" Labrey thought for a long moment. "You're sure it was a blue film?"

"I'll say. They were on the bed, very busy."

Labrey got to his feet.

"Now listen, don't say a word to anyone about this ... do you understand? Don't go yakking as you always yak." He leaned forward, his eyes glittering to stare directly into her eyes. "This is important. If you say one word to anyone, I'll fix you and you'll stay fixed!"

Vi shrank away from him, horrified by the murderous expression in his eyes.

"I won't say a thing ... honest."

"You'd better not. Stay here until I come back. Don't move from here!"

"I'll stay."

Again he stared at her for a long chilling moment, then turned and went from the room. She heard him going down the stairs three at the time.

What's happening, she thought. Oh, God! He's never been like this before! He looked as if he could kill me! Has he gone crazy? What does it all mean?

She sat there, trembling, the water from the ends of her hair making patterns on the red, soiled bedspread.

*   *   *

Although he was satisfied that he had lost Drina, Girland was still cautious. He wanted to be certain there wasn't a second tail. As Drina darted off down Rue de Vaugirard, Girland left the shop doorway and retraced his way towards Benny's studio, He spotted a free taxi, crawling in the traffic, signalled and slid in as the taxi stopped. The taxi moved off again before the cars behind could begin any impatient hooting. Girland told the driver to take him to the American Embassy.

Twenty minutes later, he walked into Mavis Paul's office. The moment she saw him, she snatched up a heavy ruler and eyed him suspiciously. She had had one embarrassing experience with him and she had no intention of repeating it.

"Hello, beautiful," Girland said, regarding the ruler and keeping his distance. "Long time no see. You're looking as radiant as this May morning. When are we going to have dinner together? I have a new and wonderful Bukhara rug I want to show you."

Mavis snapped down a switch on the intercom.

"Mr Girland is here, sir."

"Send him in." Dorey's voice was curt.

Mavis flicked her pretty fingers to the door.

"On your way, Romeo."

Girland shook his head sadly.

"If only you could realise what you are missing. A night out with me is an experience every beautiful girl dreams of."

"I can imagine," Mavis said, unimpressed. "He's waiting," and putting down the ruler where she could grab it, she continued with her typing.

"The last time you kissed me ..." Girland began but Mavis seized the ruler.

"Not another word from you!" she said, her face red. "Go in there!"

The door opened and Dorey peered into the office. "What are you waiting for, Girland? Come in ... come in," he said impatiently.

As Girland wandered into the big room, he said sadly, "It's spring and yet there is still ice around. I find it depressing."

"You leave my secretary alone," Dorey snapped. He had once caught Girland kissing Mavis and the shock still irked him. "She's a serious girl and you're wasting your time."

Girland folded himself down in the visitor's chair.

"It's never a waste of time. Where there's a will, there's a woman."

Dorey snorted and sat behind his desk.

"You are sure Drina was following you?"

"Of course." Girland took the 8mm film from his pocket and put it on the desk. "Lock it away. Now the Soviets are interested that film could be dynamite for Sherman."

"You think Drina spotted Sherman?"

"I'm sure of it." Girland reached for one of Dorey's handmade cigarettes and lit it. "I can't understand why they didn't alert the police that he was travelling on a false passport. They could have got him cold. Why follow me?"

"Kovski is a fool," Dorey said. "We can thank our lucky stars."

"Well, at least, he knows you have met Sherman and there is a film involved." Girland thought for a moment. "If Kovski thinks this is important enough – and it's my bet he will – he will put pressure on Benny Slade."

"Who's he?" Dorey demanded.

Girland told him.

"Benny had to see the film. The girl meant nothing to him. I had to show him the film to get a lead on the man who shot it. Kovski could work on Benny who is soft. If they twist his arm, he will sing. If Benny sings, Sherman is in real trouble."

Dorey considered this.

"I can't do anything official, Girland. I'm relying on you. Can you protect this man?"

"Oh, sure, but it'll cost." Girland studied Dorey. "You did say expenses, didn't you? I don't want my money frittered away."

"This is important. Spend what you like."

Girland looked at Dorey.

"I would never have expected to hear you make such a statement," he said. "Well, well ... of course it's Sherman's money you're spending, but even at that ..."

Dorey banged his fist on the desk.

"I want action and I want results! You'll be paid, but I want results."

"Take it easy. I know a couple of toughies who can take care of Benny. Instead of screaming for results, Dorey, let's have some money."

Dorey took from his drawer a thick envelope which he tossed across the desk.

"Here's ten thousand in traveller's cheques."

"Thank you ... now I can get to work."

Girland stowed the envelope away in his pocket.

"Don't lose them! They're unsigned!" Dorey hated to see Girland take so much money from him so casually.

"The way you're working yourself up, you're heading for an ulcer." Girland reached for the telephone. He spoke quietly, then replaced the receiver. "That takes care of Benny." There was a pause, then he went on, "Maybe you had better alert Sherman the Soviets are interested in him."

"How can I?" Dorey lifted his hands and slammed them down on his desk. "I can't send him a coded cable. He's never learned to decode a cable for himself. I'm cut off from him. This is unofficial, and it has to remain unofficial."

Girland stroked the end of his nose while he thought.

"I'm beginning to see now that I'll have to earn my money," he said with a crooked smile. "I'm not so sure I'm going to like this job."

"If you don't want it then give me back my money!" Dorey barked.

"I'm not as sure as all that." Girland got up and began to move to the door.

"And leave my secretary alone!" Dorey said.

"What nasty ideas come into your little mind." Girland looked sadly at Dorey, eased himself out of the room and closed the door.

At the sight of him, Mavis picked up the ruler.

Girland came slowly over to her desk, placed his hands on it and leaned towards her.

"My father told me never to be afraid of a pretty girl. Since you are the loveliest star in my sky ... kiss me."

She stared at him for a long moment, then slowly put down the ruler as Dorey opened his door.

"You still here, Girland?"

Mavis returned to her typing and Girland straightened up. He regarded Dorey with an exasperated expression.

"The only person who could ever have loved you was your mother," he said, "and I am sorry for her."

"Never mind about my mother," Dorey snapped. "You get off and earn your money."

Girland glanced at Mavis who was pounding away on her typewriter, shook his head and moved out into the corridor. As he closed the door after him, Dorey stamped back into his office.

Without pausing in her typing, Mavis smiled.

Malik sat behind his small, shabby desk and listened to what Labrey had to tell him. He thanked the gods that all his agents weren't as stupid and as unreliable as Drina. He decided this long-haired boy with his ridiculous green tinted glasses was worth five of Drina. When Drina had reported that he had lost Girland, Malik couldn't see how he was to make further progress. Now Labrey had come to him and had opened it all up again ... or rather, Labrey's girl had done so.

"Can you trust this girl?" Malik asked. His flat green eyes surveyed Labrey.

"Can you trust any woman?" Labrey shrugged. So this is Malik, he was thinking. He had heard a lot about this man from Drina, and it gave him a kick to have direct contact with him. He was everything that Labrey would wish to be: big, muscular, ruthless and very efficient. "I've thrown a scare into her, but it might not stay thrown."

"Have you anything you can use against her?"

"She steals from shops ... she's always at it."

"You have proof of this?"

"Her place is full of stolen stuff."

"That is not proof. We will have to make use of her as Girland is interested in her. Would she work for us?"

Labrey hesitated.

"I don't think so. She has no brains. She has no feeling for politics. All she thinks about is money, clothes and sex."

Malik thought for a moment: a massive stone-like figure, his huge killer hands resting on the desk.

"Then we will pay her. What do we pay you?"

"Eight hundred a month."

"We will pay her six hundred. Tell her she has no choice. Tell her we need her. If she won't co-operate, then one night something bad will happen to her ... frighten her. Make sure she understands that Russia rewards good agents, but punishes bad ones. Do you understand?"

"I understand."

"Arrange it then." Malik regarded Labrey. "I shall have further work for you. You have done well. I will see you get more money."

When Labrey had gone, Malik unlocked the bottom drawer of his desk and switched on a tape recorder. From the drawer he took a sensitive button microphone, so sensitive it didn't need leads to the recorder. He tapped the microphone gently to make sure the magic eye of the recorder reacted, then he clipped the microphone over his wristwatch and covered the watch with his frayed shirt sleeve.

He walked down the corridor to Kovski's office.

Kovski was busy writing a minute. He started violently when he saw Malik who had moved silently to Kovski's desk.

"Will you never learn to knock?" Kovski snarled, putting down his fountain pen.

Malik sat on the hard, upright chair.

"Sherman will be arriving at the Kennedy airport in another five hours," he said. "We know he is travelling on a false passport and in disguise. I understand he would not be welcomed by us as the future President. It occurred to me that you could alert the American airport police that he is travelling on a false passport."

Kovski stared at him.

"And suppose I do?"

"The police will have to take action: the Press will hear about it, there will be a scandal: Sherman won't be elected President," Malik said.

Little red patches of rage appeared on Kovski's face. Had he thought of this himself, he might have acted, but coming from Malik made this impossible as Malik had foreseen.

"Since when have you been asked to dictate policy?" Kovski demanded, his voice shaking with fury. "This is not your job! Your job is to find out why Sherman came to Paris and why Dorey has talked to Girland!"

"An anonymous cable to the American police at the Kennedy airport would result in Sherman's embarrassment," Malik said woodenly. "I suggest it is your duty to send this cable."

"Are you telling me what my duty is?" Kovski shouted.

"Yes."

Kovski glared with hatred at the big man sitting so relaxed before him.

"Be careful," he said viciously. "You are in disgrace! You are nothing! A word from me could send you for years to Siberia. You are to do what I tell you! Understand that! I will not listen to your views which are of no importance because you are stupid!" His rage so carried him away that he found he was no longer afraid of Malik.

"By sending this cable, you would be certain that Sherman could not become President of the United States," Malik said, his face expressionless.

"You think so, you fool?" Kovski snarled. "Are we so sure this man is really Sherman? We have only the word of that idiot Drina! If this man is really Sherman – and there are doubts – and we alert the American police, then how are we to find out why he came here? This is what we want to find out! As soon as the CIA know we know who he is, they will throw up a smoke-screen and then we will find out nothing!"

"We don't need to find anything out if you will send the cable. We will have achieved what we want … Sherman won't be elected President."

"You are a triple fool!" Kovski's voice was completely out of control. "How many more times do I have to tell you, idiot? What we want to know is why he came here … go and find out! As long as Sherman believes he has come

here and has got back safely to America, we have him
where we want him!"

"But we have him where we want him by sending this
cable," Malik said quietly.

"Get out!" Kovski slammed his fist down on the desk.
"Do what I tell you! Find out why Sherman has been here!
That's your job!"

A thin smile lit up Malik's stone-like face.

"Those are your orders?"

"Yes! Get out and do your job!" Malik nodded and rose
to his feet.

"I am compelled to obey your orders," he said, staring at
Kovski, "but I only obey them because you are my
superior."

He left the office, quietly, shutting the door after him and
returned to his own office. He turned off the tape recorder,
rewound the tape, listened for a few seconds to the
playback, then satisfied he had an excellent recording, he
ran off the tape. He found a large envelope and wrote on it:
*Conversation between Comrade Kovski and myself. May
5th. Subject: Henry Sherman.* He put the spool of tape into
the envelope and sealed it with Sellotape, then dropped the
envelope into his pocket. This was yet another tape to be
added to a small collection he had in a safe deposit bank
not far from the Soviet Embassy: yet another nail in Kovski's
coffin.

*　　*　　*

Still careful he wasn't being followed, Girland made his
way from the American Embassy to Pierre Rosnold's studio
on Rue Garibaldi.

The studio was housed on the fourth floor of an old-
fashioned building, but there was nothing old-fashioned
about the ornate elevator nor about Rosnold's entrance.

The double doors that led to the studio were covered with white suede, embossed with gilt scrolls and which opened automatically when Girland broke an invisible beam as he approached them. He found himself in a small lobby, draped in red velvet with gilt chairs, and a glass-topped gilt table on which were spread the usual glossy magazines.

Girland decided that Rosnold's set-up was of better taste and smelt more of money than Benny's exotic studio.

As he was surveying the scene, a door facing him opened and an elderly man, wearing a black hat and a light-grey overcoat came into the lobby. He moved with the arrogance of the very rich. In his right gloved hand, he carried a bulky envelope. His long, thin aristocratic face, the lines around the weak, sensual mouth, the smudges under his baggy eyes made him look like an ageing Casanova. His satisfied expression swiftly changed to startled apprehension as he saw Girland. He gave Girland a quick, uneasy glance, then moving quickly, he left the lobby, clutching his envelope and Girland heard him entering the elevator.

"Yes?"

Girland glanced around.

A woman stood in the doorway, regarding him. She was tall, probably in her early thirties, slim, dark with a heart-shaped face that could have been a tinted plaster mask.

"Mr Rosnold please," Girland said with his most charming smile.

The smile bounced off her like a golf ball slammed against a wall.

"Mr Rosnold is not here."

"You mean he doesn't work here any more?"

"He is not here."

"Then where do I find him?"

Again the dark eyes went over Girland, examining his clothes. From the bleak expression that showed in her eyes, the woman thought nothing of him.

"Do you want a sitting?"

The automatic doors swung open and another elderly, rich looking man came in. He hesitated for a brief moment at the sight of Girland, then gave the woman a wide, toothy smile.

"Ah, Mlle Lautre, how well you are looking." He again glanced uneasily at Girland.

The woman stood aside and smiled. The plaster mask cracked for a moment, but the smile didn't reach her eyes.

"Please go in, monsieur. I won't be a moment." The elderly man slid around her and passed through the open doorway.

"If you will give me your name, I will tell Mr Rosnold you have called."

"It's urgent. When will he be back?" Girland asked.

"Not before Monday. May I have your name?"

"It's very urgent. Where can I contact him?"

The woman stared at him. She was as hostile as a barbed-wire fence. "Your name please?"

"Tom Stag. Mr Rosnold and I have business together."

"I'll tell Mr Rosnold when he returns." The woman began to back through the doorway. "Perhaps you will telephone for an appointment on Monday," then she closed the door.

Girland left and crossed to the elevator. He thumbed the call button and while he waited, his mind was busy. When the cage stopped before him, he got in and went down to the ground floor. Before leaving the elevator, he took out his wallet and extracted two ten franc notes. He walked over to the concierge's window and tapped.

A fat, elderly woman, her hair in steel curlers, a shawl around her shoulders opened the window and regarded him with that stony, indifferent stare that most Paris concierges cultivate.

"Excuse me," Girland said and turned on charm. "I am sorry to disturb you, madame. I want to see Mr Rosnold very urgently."

"Fourth floor," the concierge snapped and prepared to shut the window.

"Perhaps you could help me." Girland put the two ten franc notes on the shelf of the window, keeping a finger on them.

The woman looked at the notes, then at Girland. She became visibly less hostile.

"I'm sure you are busy," Girland went on. "Of course, I expect to pay for your time." He took his finger off the notes. "I've already been to the fourth floor. I am told Mr Rosnold is away. I need to see him urgently. Do you happen to know where he is?"

"Didn't you ask his secretary, monsieur?" the concierge asked, eyeing the notes that lay between them.

"I did, but she was evasive. You see, madame, Mr Rosnold owes me a sum of money. If I don't find him quickly and persuade him to pay me, I shall be in trouble." Girland turned on his boyish smile. "But perhaps you can't help me." He extended his finger, but the concierge got there first. She drew the two notes out of Girland's reach and palmed them.

"I know where he is," she said, lowering her voice. "His secretary had a letter from him yesterday. I know his handwriting and the stamp interested me. The Alpenhoff Hotel, Garmisch ... that's where he is. When he left, he told me he would be away a month."

"When did he leave, madame?"

"Last Monday."

"You are very kind ... thank you, madame."

"I hope you get your money, monsieur," she said. "He is not a nice gentleman." Her old fat face crinkled into a grimace. "He is mean."

Girland again thanked her and walked out onto the busy street. He glanced at his watch. It was 16.20 hrs. He decided to visit Sammy's Bar and talk to Jack Dodge, the second lead Benny had given him.

He found Sammy's Bar on Rue Berry off Avenue des Champs Elysées: a typical, dimly lit bar like so many bars that grow like mushrooms around any tourist haunt. He pushed open the door and walked into a long narrow room, the bar to the left with the standard stools, to the right were banquettes and tables. At this hour the place was empty except for the barman who was browsing over a racing sheet, Biro in hand, a look of concentration on his handsome face.

As soon as Girland saw him, be guessed he must be Jack Dodge. This man with his sandy-coloured hair, his sun lamp complexion, his bulky shoulders and the shadow of dissipation under his close-set eyes looked the part of a stallion: a sensual lump of muscle and flesh: whose brain and mind were as small as his sexuality was enormous.

The barman glanced up, then pushed the racing sheet away. He gave Girland a smirking grin and placed big hands on the bar counter.

"Yes, sir?" he said. "What is your pleasure?"

Girland hoisted himself on a stool.

"Rye whisky and ginger ale."

"Yes, sir ... a nice reviving drink."

"That's what I need. Have one with me."

"I won't say no." The barman made two drinks with a lot of unnecessary flourishes. "First one today."

He placed one of the glasses before Girland and lifted the other.

"Santé."

They drank, then Girland asked casually, "Are you Jack Dodge?"

The barman lifted a sandy eyebrow.

"That's me. Can't say I've seen you before. I have a good memory for faces."

"That's good news. I want you to remember a girl."

"I get a lot of girls in here. I won't swear I can remember them all. It's the men I concentrate on." He grinned slyly. "They pick up the tab."

"I understand. Well, never mind about the girl for the moment. Are you still happy working for Pierre Rosnold?" Girland asked, his dark eyes on Dodge's face.

If he had leaned across the bar and punched Dodge in the eye, he wouldn't have got a bigger reaction.

Dodge reared back. His close-set eyes went blank with shock. The blood moved out of his face leaving his skin blotchy under the sun lamp complexion, but he recovered quickly. For a brief moment, when Girland could almost hear his brain creaking, he stood motionless, then pulling himself together, he eyed Girland with sudden suspicion.

"I don't know him," he said. "Excuse me. I've things to do."

"Don't be so obvious," Girland said. "You have nothing to do except talk to me. I know what your sideline is, but that doesn't mean I'll make trouble for you. How would you like to pick up an easy hundred bucks?"

"I told you, sir, I have things to do." Dodge began to move away down the bar.

"If you don't want my money, I can always call Inspector Dupuis of the vice squad and turn you in. Please yourself."

Dodge hesitated, then glared at Girland.

"Just who the hell are you?"

"Look on me as your pal," Girland said and smiled. He took ten ten-dollar bills from his wallet. These he had got by cashing some of his traveller's cheques at the American Express on his way to the bar. "All yours, buddy, for a little information which won't go further. Don't look so anxious. I'm not after you. I want to find a girl who went through a performance with you before Rosnold's camera."

Dodge eyed the money, licked his full lips, took a drink, then looked at the money again.

"You mean that's for me?"

"That's right. No strings to it ... just information."

Dodge hesitated, but the power of money was too much for him. He finished his drink, then made another while his brain creaked.

"What do you want to know?" he asked finally.

"I came across an 8 mm movie," Girland said. "It is labelled 'A Souvenir from Paris'. It shows you, wearing a hood, performing with a dark-haired girl. Three other films were shot, probably at the same time. Mean anything to you?"

Dodge again looked at the money.

"You really mean that's for me?"

Girland pushed five ten-dollar bills across the counter.

"You get the rest when you talk," he said.

Dodge snapped up the bills and stowed them away in his hip pocket.

"This is strictly confidential."

"You are right out of it," Girland promised. "What do you know about this movie?"

"Well, Rosnold called me. This was to be a special job. Okay, I make these movies. It's business and pleasure. I do a job for Rosnold two or three times a week. Last month, he called me. I went to the studio and there was this girl. I've never seen her before ... a new one." He thought for a moment. The memory seemed to please him because his face broke into a sensual leer. "Very good ... an amateur, you understand, but good."

"Did you get her name?"

Dodge shook his head.

"No. Rosnold called her Chérie, but I did get she and he were buddy-buddies. We made four films. Rosnold paid me $50 a film." Again the leer. "It was a pleasure."

"Let's do better than that," Girland said. "What makes you think Rosnold and the girl were buddies?"

"The way they behaved ... the way they talked. I could tell. I guess Rosnold digs for her."

"Yet Rosnold took the shots while you were working on her?"

"That's nothing ... that's business. I've worked with wives while their husbands took the shots. When you make a stag, it's strictly business. Besides, I got the idea the girl was stoned."

"What makes you say that?"

"Well, you know ... LSD. She was higher than a kite and as hot as a stove."

"You think she had taken LSD?"

"I'm damn sure she had."

Girland grimaced.

"What did they talk about ... did you hear anything?"

"Well ... I had to rest between the shootings." The leer irritated Girland. "While I was building myself up, they got in a huddle. They were planning to go to Garmisch together as soon as the shooting was processed."

"What do you know about Rosnold?"

Dodge shrugged.

"He's one of the bright boys. When he isn't making movies or photographing the snobs, he organises a group of nuts who call themselves Ban War. He tried to get me to join the organisation but it didn't interest me. How the hell can you ban war anyway? It's like bashing your nut against a wall. Anyway, he makes a good thing out of it. Every sucker who joins pays ten francs and the money goes into Rosnold's pocket."

The door swung open and four American tourists, each with a camera slung around his neck, came into the bar, shattering the quiet atmosphere as they climbed thirstily onto stools away from Girland.

"I see you're getting busy," Girland said. He slid the other dollar bills over to Dodge. "Forget you've seen me," and he walked out onto the street.

It now looked as if his next stop would be Garmisch, but first he wanted more information. He headed back to the American Embassy.

4

His hands clammy, his heart thumping, Henry Sherman handed his false passport to the blue-uniformed official at Orly airport. The man glanced at the photograph, glanced at Sherman, nodded, stamped the passport and returned it with a brief "Merci, monsieur."

Sherman walked through the barrier, consulted the Index board and found his flight left from Gate 10. He glanced at his watch. He had twenty-five minutes before take-off. Nice, easy time, he thought as he walked down the long aisle towards Gate 10. He paused at the bookstall to buy the *New York Times* and a couple of paperbacks, then as he was starting on his way again, there was an announcement over the tannoy.

"There will be a one hour delay on Flight AF 025 to New York. Will passengers for New York please go to the reception centre? They will be informed when to proceed to Gate 10."

Sherman flinched. This could be dangerous. The longer he remained at the airport, the greater the chances were of his being recognised.

"Tiresome, isn't it? Especially for you," a quiet voice said at his side.

Sherman started and swung around, then stiffened as he stared at the short, squat man who had come up silently and was now standing before him.

This man had hooded eyes, a thick hooked nose and the deeply tanned complexion of a man who travels a lot in the sun. He wore a black slouch hat and a dark English tweed suit, impeccably cut. Over his arm, he carried a lightweight black cashmere overcoat. A large diamond glittered in his tie. Another large diamond set in a heavy gold ring, glittered on his thick, little finger. His shirt, the handkerchief in his top pocket, his lizard skin black shoes were immaculate. He exuded power, money and luxury as he might well do for this squat man was Herman Radnitz, internationally known as one of the richest men in the world whose thick fingers spread like the tentacles of an octopus over the whole of the financial globe; a deadly spider sitting in the middle of his web moving bankers, statesmen and even minor kings as a chess player moves his pawns.

Radnitz was the last man on earth Sherman expected or wanted to see. He knew immediately that Radnitz was far too astute not to have recognised him. There was no question of attempting a bluff.

"We mustn't be seen talking together," Sherman said hurriedly. "It's too dangerous."

"Yet we will talk," Radnitz said in his guttural voice. "The door marked A." He pointed. "Go in there, I will join you."

"I am sorry, Radnitz, I ..."

"You have no alternative," Radnitz said. He paused; his hooded eyes were little pools of ice water as he stared up at Sherman. "Or do you imagine you have?"

The threat was unmistakable. Sherman only hesitated for a brief moment, then he nodded and walked away, his heart now hammering, his breathing uneven. He reached the door marked A, opened it and stepped into a luxuriously furnished waiting-room – a room, he guessed, reserved for VIPs.

A few seconds later, Radnitz joined him. He closed the door and turned the key.

"May I ask what you are doing here, Sherman?" he asked with deadly politeness. "You are travelling on a false passport and wearing a ridiculous false moustache. Are you mentally ill?"

Sherman drew himself up to his full imposing height. Although he was frightened of Radnitz, he was determined to retain his dignity. After all, he reminded himself, he was the future President of the United States. This squat German must remember this.

"I don't know what you mean! I'm perfectly well. If you are all that interested, I had to come here on urgent and private business. It was so urgent I had to resort to this – this subterfuge."

Radnitz sat down in a big lounging chair. He took a sealskin cigar case from his pocket, selected a cigar, nipped off the end of it with a gold cutter, then slowly and deliberately lit it. It was only when he was satisfied that the cigar was burning evenly that he again looked at Sherman who was now sitting on the arm of a chair opposite him, wiping his sweating face nervously with his handkerchief.

"Sufficiently urgent and sufficiently private for you to endanger your election as President of the United States?" Radnitz asked softly.

"I can't discuss this with you!" Sherman's voice was sharp. "I wouldn't be here unless it was vitally urgent."

"My dear Sherman, I think you must be forgetting our bargain." Radnitz's face was now a cold, forbidding mask. "May I remind you that the money that is making it possible for you to become the President of the United

States amounts to $35,000,000. May I also remind you that the money that is making this possible is half mine ... that I have put up half this sum from my own personal funds." He leaned forward, his eyes suddenly alight with a contained, but burning rage. "Do you imagine I will tolerate stupid behaviour from any man who owes me such a sum? Stupid behaviour? That is putting it mildly. You have been reckless and I consider the risk you have taken coming here disgraceful. If someone recognises you ... some cheap hack of a newspaperman ... anyone ... your chances of becoming President are completely and utterly damned and my money will be lost. I promised you that I would make you President. In turn, you promised me the Arcadia Dam contract. Now here you are in this ridiculous disguise here in Paris."

Sherman squirmed uneasily. It was true that he and Radnitz had made a bargain. Radnitz wanted the contract to build the Arcadia Dam ... the biggest and most expensive project on the agenda of the coming term which would cost the nation $500,000,000. Sherman had agreed that Radnitz should not only get the contract if he (Sherman) became President, but would receive five per cent of the total cost for his fee. Sherman knew that if it wasn't for Radnitz's enormous political influence and his fantastic wealth, he would not have been nominated for the Presidency in spite of his own personal wealth. So they had made the bargain.

Sherman fell back on his charm that had won over so many of his opponents, but in this small, luxury room, he realised that his charm didn't make much impact.

He forced a smile as he said, "Now, Radnitz, there is no need for you to worry. You wouldn't have known of this visit of mine but for this chance meeting ... no one else does."

"Chance? You say I wouldn't have known?" The guttural voice grated on Sherman's ears. "I knew when you left New York. I knew you were in Paris. I know you have met Dorey of the CIA. That is why I am here – two hours ahead of my flight to Rabut. I am here because I want to know why you have taken this irresponsible risk. I demand to know!"

Sherman stared at him, shrinking a little under the glaring rage that burned from the small, venomous eyes.

"You knew?" Sherman felt blood leaving his face. "I don't believe it! How could you know?"

Radnitz made a savage, impatient movement with his hand. "You are an important investment, Sherman. I have agents who are well paid to keep me informed about all my investments ... especially you. I am asking you why you are here."

Sherman licked his dry lips.

"This is a private matter. It is nothing to do with you. I can't discuss it."

Radnitz drew on his cigar. His hooded eyes never left Sherman's sweating face.

"Why did you go to Dorey and not to me?"

Sherman hesitated, then he said with an effort, "Dorey was my only hope for help. He and I have been friends for a long time ... I mean real friends."

Radnitz's thin lips curved into a pitying smile.

"So you don't consider me as a friend?"

Sherman looked directly at him, then slowly shook his head.

"No ... I look on you as a powerful associate, but not as my friend."

"So you have put your trust in a fool like Dorey?" Radnitz touched the ash off his cigar and it dropped onto the thick, green carpet. "You begin to worry me. I am now wondering if you have the personality, the authority and the necessary leadership to make for a great President." He leaned forward. "Don't you realise that if you are in urgent, personal trouble, you don't go to friends? You come to people like myself who has an investment in you and who knows how to handle any kind of trouble. So tell me ... what is this personal and urgent trouble of yours?"

"Dorey is no fool!" Sherman exclaimed. "He is handling this and I am satisfied he will produce results!"

"I asked you: what is this personal and urgent trouble? I have a right to know."

Sherman thought rapidly. Perhaps he had been irresponsible in rushing off to Paris to consult Dorey who had only been able to offer him the services of a man who Dorey had admitted was something of a crook. Maybe he (Sherman) should have consulted Radnitz and dumped the whole sordid affair in his lap, but Mary had been against consulting Radnitz. She feared and hated this fat, squat German. When Sherman had asked her if she thought he should see Radnitz, she had begged him not to. Now, although he still refused to accept Radnitz's estimate of Dorey, he began to wonder if he should have listened to his wife's advice and instead have gone immediately to Radnitz. After all, Radnitz had everything to gain in helping him and he also had tremendous influence.

Quickly, he came to a decision.

"I will tell you," he said. Briefly, he told Radnitz about the stag film, the threatening letter and also that there were three other films and his need to find his daughter.

Radnitz sat motionless, drawing on his cigar, his hooded eyes veiled while he listened.

"So you see," Sherman concluded, raising his hands helplessly. "I was desperate. Dorey is my friend. He is helping me. I had to take the risk of coming here, but now I can see I could have been hasty." He forced a smile. "I see now I should have come to you."

Radnitz let rich-smelling smoke roll out of his thin-lipped mouth.

"So Girland is handling this operation?"

Sherman regarded him.

"Sounds as if you know this man."

"There are few men of his ilk – happily few – I don't know; I once employed him with disastrous results.* He is clever, cunning and dangerous ... a man I would never trust."

"Dorey said he was my only chance to get these films."

"Yes ... I think Dorey might be right. If one pays Girland enough, he delivers. He could find the films and also your daughter." Radnitz looked quizzingly at Sherman. "Then what?"

Sherman moved uneasily.

"I will destroy the films and control my daughter."

"Will you? How old is your daughter?"

"Twenty-four."

"So how will you control her?"

"I'll reason with her ... persuade her ..."

Radnitz made an impatient movement with his hands. "What do you know about your daughter, Sherman?"

Sherman looked away, frowning, then he said slowly, "She has always been tiresome, unruly ... a rebel. I admit I don't know much about her. I haven't seen her for three years."

*see *This Is For Real*, by James Hadley Chase

"I know that. I have had her watched ... she is part of my investment." Radnitz shifted his bulk in the chair. "What are your feelings about her?"

Sherman shrugged.

"I can't say I have any great feelings about her. She just doesn't fit in with my way of life. It would be impossible to have her with us at the White House ... utterly impossible."

There was a long pause, then Radnitz said in his quiet, deadly voice, "Suppose some unfortunate accident happened to her and you lost her ... would you mind?"

Sherman stared at the squat fat man who reminded him of stone Buddha.

"I don't understand ..."

"You are wasting time!" Radnitz's voice was savage. "You heard what I asked you. If you never saw your daughter again, would you mind? That's simple enough, isn't it?"

Sherman hesitated, then slowly shook his head.

"No. In fact, it would be a relief to me if I was sure I would never see her again. But why go into this? She's here ... making a nuisance of herself, and I have to accept it."

"Do you?" Radnitz flicked ash again onto the carpet. "Your daughter presents a permanent embarrassment to you as long as she is alive. Suppose Girland is successful and he gets the films ... what good does that do you? She can make other films or she can make other scandals. The fact is she hates you and your way of life as much as you dislike her and her way of life. I have had your daughter investigated. She is tied up with this stupid, juvenile Ban War organisation. She goes around with a man called Pierre Rosnold who runs this vapid organisation for profit. She is under his influence. He is politically minded if you can call his mind a mind. She and he are determined you should not be President. He, because you stand for the escalation of the Vietnam war and because he can profit by his power: she, because you are her father and she wants revenge for the way you have neglected her." Radnitz paused to stare at Sherman. "Children have a way of paying back old scores. You wanted to be rid of her, she resented it, and now she has you where she thinks she wants you." Again Radnitz paused. "This is why," he continued, "you should have brought this problem immediately to me. Dorey may find your daughter, but he would not silence her, nor would he silence Rosnold." The ice cold eyes surveyed Sherman. "But I would and can."

Sherman felt sweat break out on his forehead.

"I can't listen to this kind of talk," he said. "I am sure you don't mean what you seem to be suggesting."

"What other solution is there to this problem?" Radnitz asked. "Suggest something. Girland will probably find your daughter ... then what?"

Sherman had no answer to this. He gnawed his lip, staring down at the carpet.

"Are you going to allow a degenerate chit of a girl to stand between you and the White House?" Radnitz asked. "Because of the way you have treated her in the past, she will stop at nothing to prevent you becoming President and she has the power to do this if she is allowed to. These films can be found and destroyed ... they are nothing. It is not the films that need to be destroyed ... it is she."

A voice broke in on this conversation, coming through the loudspeaker on the wall.

"Passengers for Flight 025 to New York should now proceed to Gate 10. Thank you."

Sherman got hastily to his feet.

"I must go," he said huskily. He looked at Radnitz for a brief, furtive moment, then looked away. "I feel sure I can leave this in your hands ..."

But Radnitz wasn't going to let this tall, white-faced future President of the United States off his hook, nor let him shift his responsibilities nor let him salve his conscience so easily.

"I am going to cancel my flight," he said. "I am at the Georges V hotel. When you get home, telephone Dorey and find out what is happening. Then telephone me. Is that understood?"

Sherman nodded and began edging to the door.

"One moment ..." The ice cold eyes surveyed Sherman. "I am to take it that I can arrange to get rid of your daughter?"

Sherman swallowed and dabbed his face with his handkerchief.

"I – I must discuss it with Mary ... but if you think there is no other alternative ... I – I suppose I must leave it to you. Gillian has always ..." He stopped with a shudder. "I must go."

"Very well then, I will wait to hear from you. It is your responsibility. I will act if you say so."

As Sherman hurried from the room, Radnitz made a grimace of contempt.

*   *   *

Vi sat on the bed, her eyes round as she listened to what Labrey was saying. He was sitting in the shabby armchair, facing her, a cigarette between his nicotine-stained fingers, his eyes glittering behind the green glasses.

At first she thought he was joking, but now she realised he was serious. As he talked on, she felt a cold chill of fear crawling over her. Paul! Working for the Russians! She had a childlike terror of anything to do with the Russians. She had seen all the James Bond films. She had adored Michael Caine in his spy films. She had read about Philby and Blake. Spies fascinated her so long as they remained on the screen or in newspapers or in books, but now Paul was telling her she was committed ... suddenly she was a spy for Russia!

"I won't do it!" she said fiercely. "I won't have anything to do with it! Take your things and get out! Now ... do you hear? This very minute!"

"Oh, shut up!" Labrey said wearily. "You're going to do what I tell you! You've only got yourself to blame for this because you have hot pants. If you had left Girland alone, you wouldn't be in this mess. Now you've got to make yourself useful."

"Girland?" Bewildered, Vi clutched her wrap close to her. "What has he to do with this?"

"Don't be so goddamn dumb! Girland is an agent as I am. You're meeting him tonight. We want to know what he is up to, and you are going to find out!"

"Then I won't meet him! A spy? Is he a spy? I'm not having anything to do with this! You pack your things and get out!"

"My boss has decided you are going to work for us," Labrey said quietly. "He has decided, so you will work for us or else ..." He paused, staring at her through his green tinted glasses.

Vi shivered. The quietness of his voice was much more effective than if he had shouted at her. She was used to men shouting and getting into rages. During her short experience as a prostitute, so many men had shouted at her and she had learned how to handle them, but this quiet, deadly voice terrified her.

"Or else ... what?" she asked, her voice quavering.

"They have a technique with women who won't co-operate," Labrey said. "Women are easy. You can't hope to run away and hide. Sooner or later, wherever you are, they will find you. There are two things they can do: you are walking along some street and a man appears. He has a spray gun of acid. You get the acid in your face, and your flesh peels off the way you skin an orange. That is one thing they can do. The other is they grab you and shove you in a car and take you to some house they have rented. Then they do things to you. I don't know just what they do ... I haven't bothered to ask, but the girls after the treatment, don't walk well." He stared at her. "They have to keep their legs apart as they walk ... so they hobble. I've heard girls prefer the acid to the other treatment ..."

Vi regarded him in horror.

"I don't believe it! You're trying to frighten me!"

Labrey got to his feet.

"Think about it. Turn it over in your little mind. I'm not trying to frighten you. I'm sorry for you. You have a hook in your mouth now ... and it won't come out. You will go to this restaurant and meet Girland tonight. You will find out what he is planning to do. If you don't find out, you will get the treatment. Nothing can save you. You can run, but they will always find you. So think about it."

He left the sordid little room and taking the stairs three at a time, he made his way down to the street.

*　　*　　*

Girland eased open the door leading to Mavis Paul's office and moved silently into the room. If he had hoped to catch Dorey's pretty secretary unawares, he was disappointed. She was about to enter Dorey's office and she had the door half open.

"You again?" she said with a half-smile. She stepped into Dorey's office, leaving the door wide open. "Mr Girland is here, sir."

"Send him right in," Dorey said, laying down his pen and pushing aside a file.

Girland entered the big room, giving Mavis a suggestive wink which she ignored.

"Would you please do something for me?" he said pausing. "Would you get the Alpenhoff Hotel at Garmisch on the phone for me?"

Mavis looked questioningly at Dorey who nodded.

"Right away," she said and giving Girland a wide berth, she left the room.

Girland came over and helped himself to one of Dorey's cigarettes. He sat on the arm of the visitor's chair and lit the cigarette.

"I'm making progress. I wanted to check with you. What do you know about Ban War ... an organisation?"

Dorey shrugged.

"It's like the rest of them ... they have about five thousand members ... most of them young. Their headquarters is in a cellar club on the Left Bank. I'd say they are pretty harmless. They throw the occasional brick, squat in the streets, paint signs on the walls and generally enjoy themselves. They are no more violent, no more vicious than the rest of the antibrigades."

"Gillian Sherman is a member." Girland went on to tell Dorey what he had learned that afternoon. "So it would seem that Rosnold and Gillian have gone off to Garmisch. I'm catching the 07.50 flight to Munich tomorrow. From there I'll hire a car and drive to Garmisch." He tapped ash into Dorey's ashtray. "I could catch up with this girl ... just what do I do with her if I do catch up with her?"

"You are to persuade her to give you the other three films and make her come back with you to Paris. You are to bring her to me. I'll then arrange for her to be sent home."

Girland lifted his eyebrows.

"Suppose she tells me to jump into a lake ... what then?"

Dorey moved impatiently.

"This is part of your job, Girland. You are free to offer her any reasonable sum of money if she will co-operate. Sherman doesn't care what this costs so long as he gets the films and gets his daughter home."

"Has it crossed Sherman's small mind that she might not give a damn about money?"

Dorey stiffened.

"That's no way to talk about your future President, Girland. Don't you realise this is a national emergency?"

Girland laughed.

"Oh, come on! It isn't. It's Sherman's emergency. I dare say the American public could easily find another President. But why should I care? Suppose she isn't interested in money? There are still some people who aren't interested in money ... odd as it seems. Do you authorise me to kidnap her?"

"I am paying you twenty thousand dollars to bring this girl here and get those films! I don't wish to discuss how you will do it ... do it!"

There came a tap on the door and Mavis looked in.

"I have the Alpenhoff Hotel on the line," she said and withdrew.

Girland picked up the telephone receiver on Dorey's desk.

"Reception, please," he said, then went on, "Is Mr Pierre Rosnold staying with you?" He listened, then said, "No, thank you. I just wanted to be sure he is still with you. Will you reserve a single room with bath for me for tomorrow … three or four days. Mark Girland. Fine … thank you," and he hung up. "He's still there," he said to Dorey, "and I imagine she'll be there too."

"Can't you get off tonight?"

Girland shook his head.

"Too late tonight." He was thinking of his date with Vi Martin. He believed in pleasure before business. "I'll get off first thing tomorrow morning. I'll be in Munich by 9.15, pick up a Hertz car at the airport and be in Garmisch by 11.30. Can you get your secretary to book me on the 07.50 flight?"

"Of course. Your ticket will be waiting for you at the airport."

"Then I'll get along."

"Keep me informed and be careful."

As Girland started for the door, Dorey said, "There's one thing you should know … Malik is in Paris."

This news stopped Girland in his tracks.

"I thought he was in Moscow, standing in a corner with a dunce cap on his head."

"He's in Paris, but he is probably standing in a corner. Knowing Kovski, he could turn Malik onto this if they really mean to make trouble for Sherman."

"That would make this job a real beauty," Girland said. "Well, okay, thanks for telling me."

Dorey got to his feet and walked with Girland to the door. He stood in the doorway as Girland passed Mavis who didn't look up from her typing. Aware Dorey was watching him, Girland kept on his way down to the street.

He took a taxi to Benny Slade's studio, made sure that the two guards he had hired were on the job, then he collected his car and drove back to his apartment. He didn't bother to check to see if he was being followed. The time to make sure he wasn't being followed was when he set off for Orly airport the following morning. Now, he could relax, reserve a table at Chez Garin, pack a bag, take a shower, have a couple of drinks, then stretch out on his bed until it was time to meet Vi Martin.

A few minutes to 21.00 hrs, Girland arrived at Chez Garin restaurant to be welcomed by Georges Garin who, before coming to Paris, had lived for some years in Nuits-St Georges where the truly great Burgundy wines are born.

As Girland was settling at his table, Vi arrived. The moment he saw her approaching him, he knew something was wrong. The unnatural glitter in her eyes and her quick grimace of a smile as he got to his feet made him wonder if she wasn't loaded with pep pills. He was disappointed. There was now something about her that made her less attractive, less sexually exciting than when he had first seen her.

She further dampened his spirits by declaring she wasn't hungry. He had hoped that she would have enjoyed the décor of this gracious restaurant, but she didn't look around her so when Garin joined them, Girland explained that Mademoiselle would prefer something very light. Garin suggested his *truite soufflé*, explaining the trout was first boned, then stuffed with the pounded flesh of a pike. The trout was cooked in butter and served with a butter sauce to which was added almonds and raisins.

Watching her, Girland saw Vi cringe as Garin explained the dish, but she said quickly it sounded marvellous and she would have it. Feeling even more depressed, Girland ordered a *steak au poivre en chemise*. Garin suggested a slice of smoked salmon with buttered shrimps to begin the meal.

Vi was hipped up. Terrified by Labrey's threats, she had decided to do what he told her to do. To get herself into the right mood, she had taken four Purple Heart pills before leaving her room. Their effect made her now feel light-headed, reckless but queasy. Somehow she managed to eat the smoked salmon. She prattled to Girland about Benny, her modelling work, what a gorgeous restaurant this was, about the movies she had seen in a non-stop flow that quickly got on Girland's nerves.

Well, you can't expect to pick them all the time, he thought as he toyed with his glass of Chablis. She looked marvellous. Now she was hipped to her eyeballs, and for God's sake, woman! do stop this awful yakkiting!

Suddenly aware that she was boring him and suddenly terrified that she was handling this badly, Vi pulled herself together.

"But tell me about yourself," she gushed. "I want to know all about you … everything. How do you manage to live so well and not work?"

The *truite soufflé* and the *steak au poivre* arrived at this moment and Girland paused to discuss with Garin what Burgundy he should have with his steak. Having decided on a Nuits-St Georges 1949 which he knew would cost him enormously, but felt he deserved as a compensation for having being landed with this yakking girl, he turned his attention once more to her – this blonde beauty who was now overwhelming him with her gushing interest in his way of life.

"I wouldn't say I live well," Girland said. "I get along. I've lived in Paris now for fifteen years. There are plenty of ways of making money here and there if you know the right people and know what to do."

Vi pushed her trout about on her plate with her fork. She couldn't bring herself to eat it. The pills were now making her feel bad.

"That sounds marvellous." She patted his hand and smiled at him. "For instance, tell me, what are you doing tomorrow?"

Completely bored with her now, Girland glanced at his watch.

"This time tomorrow I will be in Garmisch," he said. "I have a little deal on there."

"Garmisch? How wonderful! What kind of deal?"

Girland regarded her thoughtfully, then grinned.

"Oh, a deal. What are you doing tomorrow?"

"I'm modelling for Benny."

Garmisch! Vi was thinking, aware that she was now feeling sick. She swallowed the rising saliva back. Garmisch! This was what Paul wanted to know! Well, at least, she had learned something. She could see Girland was disappointed in her, and she couldn't blame him. Paul had said he was an agent. She was scared to ask further questions. She could make him suspicious.

All the fun and joy had gone out of her life now. She remembered Paul's threat: *You now have a hook in your mouth … and it won't come out.* The terror that was gnawing at her had ruined her evening. She had been crazy to have taken so many of those damned pills. Now the sight of the *truite soufflé* suddenly turned her stomach.

She felt if she didn't get out at once, she would disgrace herself. She turned desperately to Girland, her face pallid, little beads of sweat on her upper lip.

"I'm terribly sorry ... I'm not well ... I – I have this awful liver thing ... it hits me ..." She got hastily to her feet. "I – forgive me ... I'm so sorry ..."

Seeing her obvious distress, Girland moved quickly, taking her arm and leading her to the lobby. Garin came to his side.

"A taxi," Girland said. "Mademoiselle is not well."

There was a taxi waiting by the time Vi had put on her coat.

"I want to go home alone," she said to Girland. She couldn't bear another second of his company so great was her terror. "Thank you ... I'm sorry ..."

"But of course I'll take you home," Girland said quietly.

Vi cried hysterically, "I want to go alone! Leave me alone!" Pushing past Girland, she ran out, got into the taxi and was driven away.

Girland stared after the taxi, then shrugged.

You can't win all the time, he told himself as he walked back to his table, feeling depressed. His evening had collapsed under him.

The *steak au poivre* had been removed and was being kept hot. The wine waiter served the Burgundy. Girland received his steak, but he now found he had lost his appetite. A gruesome evening, he thought, but cheered up slightly after drinking a glass of the magnificent wine.

Later, he left the restaurant and got into his little Fiat. He sat for a long moment wondering what to do. The time now was 21.50 hrs. He wondered if he should go to the Poker Club where the game would be in full swing, but decided against it. He wasn't in the mood, and besides, he reminded himself he would have to be up horribly early to catch the 07.50 flight to Munich. Feeling deflated, he decided to return to his apartment.

One of these days, he said to himself as he drove with the slow moving traffic, you'll have to find yourself a permanent woman. You're getting bored with looking after yourself ... chasing rainbows.

He became even more gloomy with this thought until suddenly he caught sight of a blonde girl running along the sidewalk. She wore a red mini skirt and a tight-fitting white sweater. She ran easily and well, and her long legs were slim and beautiful: her full breasts bounced joyfully as she ran.

Girland brightened immediately. So long as there were girls around like this one, he told himself, there must still be fun and hope left in this drab, drab world.

In a much better frame of mind, he continued on towards his apartment.

* * *

Vi lay on the bed. She was feeling better. She had only just managed to reach the toilet on the eighth floor before she had thrown up. She was now feeling relaxed, a little cold and still frightened, but better. She began to think of that delicious looking trout left on the plate at Chez Garin and became aware she was hungry.

The door jerked open and Labrey came in. He stood in the doorway glaring at her.

"What the hell are you doing back here?" he snarled. He moved into the tiny room and slammed the door. "Why aren't you with Girland?"

Vi cringed away from him.

"I was ill ... I did see him ... I took too many pills. I had to leave."

Labrey stood over her. He looked as if he were about to hit her.

"Ill? Didn't you find out anything, you stupid bitch?"

"Don't call me that!" Vi struggled to sit upright, but he put his hand over her face and slammed her back on the pillow.

"Answer me!"

"He told me he was going to Garmisch tomorrow."

Labrey drew in a long, deep breath, then sat on the bed beside her. He put his hand on her arm, digging his fingers into her flesh.

"Garmisch, Germany? Are you sure?"

"How can I be sure? ... he told me he was ... you're hurting me!"

"What happened? Tell me everything!"

As he released the grip on her arm, Vi recounted the meeting at the restaurant and what was said.

Labrey considered what she had told him, then got to his feet.

"All right. Stay here. I must telephone."

"But I'm hungry," Vi wailed.

"Then come with me. I want to eat too."

As Vi struggled off the bed, she asked, "Have I done right? Are you pleased with me?"

He suddenly smiled at her. The hateful, savage expression went off his face and he was again the Paul she knew.

"You've done damn well ... at least, I think so. Come on, let's get out of here."

At the bistro on Rue Lekain, Labrey left her to order the meal while he shut himself into the telephone booth. He got through to the Soviet Embassy and asked for Malik. Although it was now 21.30 hrs, Malik was still at his desk, plodding through the mass of paperwork Kovski had left him.

Labrey reported that Girland was going to Garmisch the following morning.

"Hold on," Malik said. There was a long pause, then he came back on the line. "There is only one morning flight to Munich at 07.50. The next flight is at 14.00 hrs. Girland will take the first flight. You are to travel with him. Find out where he is staying. Be careful. This man is very dangerous. I will follow on the next flight. Girland knows me. I can't travel with him. I will wait for you at the Garmisch railway station. Do you understand?"

"Yes."

"Your girl is to come with me ... she might be useful. Tell her to be at Orly airport at 01.15 hrs. How will I know her?"

Labrey stiffened.

"She won't come ... she's difficult."

"She is to come. Arrange it." The snap in Malik's voice warned Labrey there was to be no further argument. "How will I recognise her?"

"She has blonde hair down to her shoulders. I will tell her to carry a copy of *Paris Match*."

"Very well. She is to be waiting outside Hertz Rental car office at Orly at 01.15 hrs. Your ticket to Munich will be at Air France's information desk. You understand what you have to do and where to meet me?"

"Yes. Then tomorrow," and Malik hung up.

Labrey stood for a long moment in the kiosk, then bracing himself, he walked back to where Vi was eating onion soup. He sat down and began on his own onion soup.

She looked up, lifting her eyebrows.

"Now what's happening?"

He told her that she was to meet Malik at Orly and fly with him to Munich. Vi stared at him, blood leaving her face.

"No! I won't do it!" she said, pushing aside the soup.

Labrey expected this reaction. He shrugged and went on eating.

"All right," he said, without looking at her. "I've warned you. If you won't do it ... you take the consequences. They never take no for an answer ... you either do what you are told or you get the treatment."

Vi shivered.

"Eat up!" Labrey said. "You told me you were hungry."

"Paul! How could you do this to me?" she said, tears in her eyes. "How could you?"

Labrey stared at her coldly.

"I've done nothing." He stirred the soup as he continued to stare at her. "You went after Girland. If you hadn't such hot pants for any man with money you wouldn't be in this mess. Don't blame me. But you went after him, now you have a hook in your mouth. It won't and can't come out. I'm sorry for you. You either do what you are told or you'll get the treatment."

"I'll go to the police!" Vi said desperately. "They'll protect me!"

"Do you think so?" Labrey shrugged and finished his soup. "Okay, go ahead and tell them. What can they do? Do you imagine they will give you a flic to walk behind you for months? You can't get away. You're hooked. You either do what they tell you or they will peel the skin off your face or shove a wedge between your legs."

Vi sat for a long moment, her eyes closed, her hands clenched into fists on the table, then she pushed back her chair and got up.

"I'll go back and pack a bag," she said. "I can't eat any more."

When she had gone, Labrey grimaced. He too had lost his appetite. When the waiter brought him a steak, he waved it away.

5

Mary Sherman was tall and elegant: a woman in her early forties. She looked as if she had stepped out of a Beaton photograph: immaculately dressed by Balmain, she was extremely conscious that before long she would be the First Lady of the United States. She was a shrewd, cold and calculating woman with a burning ambition for her husband and herself. She had a cold, magnetic charm. She seemed to have an irresistible interest in people who felt, when they met her, that their cares were her cares: it was a trick that served her husband well.

As Sherman came into the big, comfortable lounge, Mary was at her desk, writing a letter. She turned, looked inquiringly at him with those blue, impersonal eyes and then got to her feet.

"Henry! I've been waiting." She moved to him and kissed his unshaven cheek with a little grimace of disapproval. "Was it all right? What happened?"

During the drive back to Washington from Kennedy airport, Sherman had got rid of his false moustache, but he had retained the heavy sun goggles. He had picked up his car which he had left at the airport, but his return hadn't been so lucky as his leaving. As he had come in through the back entrance to his imposing house, Morgan, one of the FBI agents responsible for his security, had stepped out of the shadows. The two men had confronted each other, genuine horror in Morgan's eyes.

Sherman realised Morgan's position and he gave him his wide, easy smile, strictly reserved for the people who might vote for him.

"I felt like a breath of fresh air, Morgan," he said, "so I slipped out. I'm feeling fine now." He put his hand on Morgan's arm, patting it as he had patted so many arms of possible voters. "Naughty of me ... I'm sorry. Let's keep it between ourselves, huh?" Then before the horrified agent could protest, Sherman had left him and had entered the house.

"Morgan spotted me as I was coming in," Sherman said, stripping off his overcoat, "but it's more than his job's worth to report it." He dropped wearily into an armchair. "Sit down, Mary ... let me tell you."

She sat by his side.

"Have you found her?"

"Not yet." Sherman went on to tell her about his talk with Dorey and what Dorey was doing.

Mary listened to this, her eyes incredulous.

"You mean there is only this ex-agent looking for her?" she exclaimed. "This is ridiculous, Henry! Why didn't you consult the police?"

"And make this official?" Sherman shook his head. "Use your brains! We have no choice but to hope Dorey's man will find her."

"A crook! Henry!"

He looked at her.

"We have to find her, Mary ... this man will find her."

She made a savage little movement with her hands.

"And then ... what?"

"It is possible he will be able to persuade her ..."

"Oh, for God's sake! Persuade her? Gillian? How can any man persuade a little fiend like that!" She got to her feet and began to move around the big room, beating her fists together. "Can't you realise she is determined to ruin us! Why did I have to produce such a child! Listen, Henry ... you must give up the election. At least, if you withdraw, we can keep our social life intact, but once those filthy films get into the wrong hands ... how can we face anyone and who would want to see us again?"

Sherman got wearily to his feet. He crossed over to the telephone, consulted his pocket address book, then dialled Dorey's home number in Paris.

"Who are you calling?" Mary demanded shrilly.

"Dorey. He may have news for us."

Dorey was in bed, asleep, when the sound of the telephone bell woke him. He became instantly awake and alert.

"Is that you, Dorey?" He recognised Sherman's voice.

"Yes ... you've got back all right?"

"All right ... have you any news for me?"

"Yes ... some good ... some bad. I must be careful. We are talking over an open line." There was a pause, then he went on, "You remember Uncle Joe?"

Sherman stiffened.

"Of course ... what is this, John?"

"His nephews are now interested. Mr Cain was recognised as he left Orly. Joe's nephews know Mr Cain and I met."

Sherman's face went slack with shock. Watching him, Mary jumped to her feet in alarm.

"What is it, Henry?"

He waved her to silence.

"Do they know about the movie?" he asked Dorey.

"I don't think so, but they are curious. My man has been alerted."

"Well, go on ... what else?"

"My man is going to Garmisch ... he should be on his way in an hour or so," Dorey said. "He has received information that the party you are interested in is there."

"Garmisch ... Germany? Are you sure?"

"Yes. The party is staying at the Alpenhoff Hotel."

"Do you think your man can handle this?"

"If he can't, no one can."

"Then I suppose I must accept this situation ... I'm not happy about it, but I am relying on you."

"I will do my best, sir." Dorey's voice sounded flat. Sherman's obvious lack of confidence hurt him. "I will telephone you again," and he hung up.

Sherman slowly replaced the receiver and then turned and looked at Mary.

"A Russian agent recognised me at Orly and now the Russians are on to this."

Mary's hand went to her mouth; her face became waxen. "You mean they know about these filthy films?"

"Not yet, but they are investigating. This man Girland has located Gillian at the Alpenhoff Hotel, Garmisch."

"Garmisch? What is she doing there?"

Sherman shrugged impatiently.

"How do I know? Girland is on his way there now."

Mary suddenly pounded her clenched fists on the back of the settee.

"What can a man like that do? God! I wish the little bitch was dead!"

Sherman shifted uneasily.

"You'd better know, Mary ... I ran into Radnitz in Paris ... of course, he recognised me."

Mary stared at him, her steel-blue eyes widening.

"Radnitz? He recognised you?"

"Yes. It was one of those things ... I told him what was happening."

"You mean you told him about Gillian and these filthy films?"

"I had no alternative."

Mary dropped onto the settee.

"Henry! Radnitz only thinks about this contract! You were mad to have told him. Now he will blackmail you!"

Sherman looked patiently at her.

"You're being stupid. Radnitz can't expect the contract unless I am President. He is ready to help me." He crossed to the cocktail cabinet, made himself a stiff whisky and soda, then came and sat down again.

"Radnitz help you?" Mary's voice was shrill. "You can't believe a man like that would help anyone!"

"Mary ... just a moment ago you said you wished Gillian was dead ... do you mean that?" Sherman asked, not looking at her.

She sensed the question was serious. For a long moment, she sat still, her face expressionless.

Finally, she said, "If she was dead, you would become the President of the United States. If she remains alive and continues to blackmail us, you won't become the President ... so ... yes ... I suppose I do wish she was dead."

Sherman stared down at his hands.

"Radnitz said the same thing. He said he could arrange it. I – I told him to go ahead ... I was worked up, but before he takes action, I wanted to talk to you ... then if you agree, I have to tell him where to find her." He stroked the back of his neck, staring out of the window. "He knows where she is, of course. He knows everything, but if I tell him she is at the Alpenhoff Hotel at Garmisch, he will know this is my okay for him to get rid of her."

Mary leaned forward, her eyes glittering.

"Well, what are you waiting for?" she demanded. "We have fought and fought to come this far. Why should our ambitions and our way of life be ruined because we have been unlucky enough to have spawned this hateful, spiteful animal. Call Radnitz and tell him where she is!"

Sherman moved in his chair. His shaking hands went over his sweating face.

"She is our daughter, Mary."

"Call him!"

They stared at each other for a long moment, then Sherman shook his head.

"No! We can't do this, Mary. We can't!"

"And the Russians? Suppose they find out about this degenerate animal? We can't allow ourselves to be blackmailed by such a creature. She must be silenced!"

Sherman made a helpless gesture.

"Suppose we wait until Girland finds her. He might just possibly talk some sense into her." He got to his feet. "I'm going to bed."

"Yes ..." Mary looked strangely at him. Her eyes were remote. "The Alpenhoff Hotel, Garmisch ... you said?"

"Yes."

"And where is Radnitz?"

Sherman hesitated.

"Georges V, Paris." He looked away from her. "Why do you ask?"

"Go to bed, Henry," Mary said quietly. "You need your rest."

Sherman hesitated again, then moved to the door. He paused and looked at her. Her cold, hard eyes fixed his.

"Go to bed, Henry," she repeated.

Sherman left the lounge. He moved slowly like an old man moving to his bed, directed by his nurse. She listened to him mount the stairs and the slight creak of the floorboards as he moved into his bedroom.

For sometime, she sat staring out of the window, watching the sun rising, heralding a new day. Her face was stony, only the glitter in her eyes hinted at the turmoil that was going on in her mind.

Finally, she reached for the telephone. She asked the operator to connect her with Georges V hotel, Paris.

* * *

A black Thunderbird drew up under the canopy of the Georges V hotel and the doorman stepped forward to open the car door.

Lu Silk slid out.

"Park it ... I won't be long," he said curtly and walked into the lobby. He crossed to the concierge who was standing behind his desk.

"Mr Radnitz," Silk said.

The concierge had seen Silk several times. He knew him to be a man who didn't tip and was disagreeable to the staff.

The concierge inclined his head coldly, picked up a telephone receiver, spoke briefly, then said to Silk, "Fourth floor, monsieur, suite 457."

Silk sneered at him.

"As if I didn't know." He turned and walked towards the elevators.

Lu Silk* was Herman Radnitz's professional killer: a tall, lean man in his early forties with a hatchet-shaped face, a

---

* see *Believed Violent*, by James Hadley Chase.

glass left eye and a white scar running down the side of his left cheek. His crew-cut hair was white. He wore a dark flannel suit that fitted him well, and he carried a black slouch hat in his hand. He had worked for Radnitz now for some years. When Radnitz wished to get rid of anyone troublesome, he called for Silk. For $15,000 as a killing fee and $30,000 as a yearly retainer whether he worked or not, Lu Silk made a satisfactory living.

He arrived on the fourth floor and rang the bell of suite 457. The door was opened by Ko-Yu, Radnitz's Japanese servant and chauffeur.

"Hi," Silk said as he entered. "The old man waiting for me?"

Ko-Yu regarded Silk, his face expressionless, his manner distant.

"Mr Radnitz is expecting you."

Silk went into the big, luxuriously furnished sitting-room where Radnitz was at his desk, dictating to his secretary, Fritz Kurt, a small, thin man who glanced up as Silk came in.

Radnitz broke off his dictation and waved Kurt away. There was a moment's pause while Kurt left the room, then Radnitz said, "I have work for you."

"That's easy to guess." Silk was in awe of no man, and he never showed any respect when talking to Radnitz. He was the only member of Radnitz's staff who wasn't a "Yes-man". He sat down and crossed one leg over the other. "Who is it this time?"

"You are ready to travel immediately?"

"Of course. I always keep a bag in the car. Where to?"

"Munich." Radnitz opened a briefcase and took from it a bulky envelope. "Here are your instructions with your ticket and travellers cheques. You are to get rid of two people. A girl: Gillian Sherman. A man: Pierre Rosnold. There is a photograph of the girl here, but I have no photograph of the man, but they will be together. This is important, Silk. You will receive thirty thousand dollars when I know they have been eliminated."

Silk got up, crossed to the desk and took the envelope Radnitz was offering him. He returned to his chair, sat down and removed the contents of the envelope. He paused to study the photograph of Gillian Sherman. Her beauty had no effect on him. For more years than he could remember, Silk had lost interest in women. He read through two typewritten pages of instructions, then he looked up.

"I don't hit them until these films are recovered? How do I know when they are recovered?"

"This man Girland will get them. He will be constantly watched. You don't have to worry about that. Your job is to get rid of these two when you are told to go ahead."

"How do you want this arranged?"

Radnitz selected a cigar from a cedar, gold-topped box.

"An accident ... perhaps a hunting accident?"

"The two of them?"

Silk shook his head.

"No ... one of them could be shot by mistake, but not two of them. The German police aren't stupid."

Radnitz shrugged impatiently. Small details always bored him.

"I leave it to you. I have a place near Oberammergau. I have a good man there and I have already alerted him. He will do everything that is necessary. His name is Count Hans von Goltz. You will be met at the Munich airport and taken to my place. By that time, von Goltz will have information for you. You need take no weapons. There is everything you may need at my place. I have some thirty

106

good men who look after the estate. You can use them if you want them."

Silk put the envelope in his pocket and got to his feet.

"I'd better get off if I'm to catch the 14.00 hr plane."

"Be careful of Girland," Radnitz warned. "He is dangerous."

Silk showed his even white teeth in a vicious smile.

"I'll watch it," he said and left the suite.

Because Mary Sherman had forgotten to tell Radnitz that now the Russians were also involved in this hunt for the daughter of the future President, Silk left the Georges V hotel thinking he had only Girland to deal with. Had he known that he was to come up against not only Girland, but Malik as well, he would have been less confident he was on to easy money as he drove his Thunderbird towards Orly airport.

*   *   *

Feeling slightly jaded, Girland passed through the Customs barrier at the Munich airport and made his way across the big hall to the Hertz Rental car service. Seeing where he was going, Labrey, who had been following him, paused. He had little money to spare. There was no question of his hiring a car. His Soviet masters were tight with money. He watched Girland as he talked to the girl clerk.

Girland showed his Hertz Credit Card and told the girl, a pretty blonde, he wanted a Mercedes 230.

"Yes, sir," the girl said. "How long will you need it, do you think?"

"I don't know." Girland found the girl attractive. "It depends on how much I like your country. If it's as lovely as you are, I might spend the rest of my days here."

The girl giggled and blushed. "Shall we say ... a week?"

"Leave it open ... I don't know." Girland leaned on the counter while she completed the form, then he signed it.

"I'll get the car for you, sir." She used the telephone and then hung up. "In five minutes, sir." She looked adoringly at him as she smiled. "The exit door is to your right."

"Thank you."

They exchanged glances, then feeling considerably revitalised, Girland left the airport and stood waiting in the pale sunshine for the car to arrive.

"Excuse me, sir," a voice said at his side. "Would you be going to Garmisch?"

Girland turned. Standing by his side was a tall, thin young man with long blond hair and wearing green tinted sunglasses. He had a rucksack on his back.

"Sure," Girland said. "Do you want a lift?"

"I was hoping for one," Labrey said, "but I don't want to push myself onto you."

At this moment a black Mercedes pulled up beside them. The white coated driver got out and saluted Girland.

"You understand the car, sir?"

"Oh, sure." Girland tossed his suitcase onto the back seat. He tipped the man, then turning to Labrey, he went on, "Hop in."

Labrey slid into the passenger's seat. He put the rucksack down between his feet.

Girland got under the driving wheel and set the car in motion.

Labrey said, "Thank you very much, sir." The conversation from the beginning had been in French. "You're an American, aren't you?"

"That's right."

"You look American, but your French is perfect."

"I guess I get by. Where are you from?" Girland asked as he headed the car fast along the highway towards Munich.

"I'm from Paris. I'm on vacation. I plan to walk through the Isar valley to Bad Tolz," Labrey said. He had spent his time profitably while in the aircraft, reading a guide book of Germany which he had bought at Orly airport.

"Fine walking country," Girland said.

Labrey looked shiftily at him.

"Are you on vacation or on business, sir?"

"A bit of both. You're walking from Garmisch?"

"Yes, but I will stay in Garmisch for a few days if I can find a cheap hotel."

"You won't have any trouble about that. There are plenty of good, cheap hotels to choose from." Girland spoke from experience as he often came to Garmisch for the winter sports.

Having been warned by Malik about Girland, Labrey decided not to ask any further questions. It was truly a bit of luck to be riding with this ex-CIA agent who obviously was quite unsuspecting. Labrey was pleased with himself.

The conversation got around to Paris and the nightclubs. Labrey could tell Girland of two or three he didn't know and Girland could tell Labrey of a dozen and more he didn't know. Chatting this way, they reached Munich and Girland who knew the route, took the outer-ring road and got onto E.6 highway that led directly to Garmisch, under 100 kilometres from Munich. Once on this highway, Girland increased speed and within a little over an hour and a half, he drove into Garmisch's crowded, narrow main street.

Pulling up by the square, he said, "You'll find three or four hotels over there to the left."

"Are you going to one of them?" Labrey asked as he opened the car door.

"My hotel's further down the road." Girland offered his hand. "Have a good vacation."

"Thanks for the ride, sir."

Girland nodded, started the car moving and drove on to the Alpenhoff Hotel. Labrey half ran, half walked after the Mercedes which was moving slowly as the traffic was heavy. He saw Girland swing the car into the driveway of the hotel, then satisfied he knew where Girland was staying, he went in search of a cheap hotel for himself.

As Girland walked into the softly lit hotel lobby, a short, chunky man, wearing a canary coloured polo neck sweater and white slacks paused to let him pass. Behind him was a girl who Girland immediately recognised as Gillian Sherman from the movie he had seen. He was sure he wasn't mistaken. She was slightly above average height. Her bronze-coloured hair was cut in the shape of a helmet which suited her attractive, sun-tanned face. She had on a white square-necked sweater and black stretch-pants, revealing her sensual figure.

Girland immediately stopped and stood aside to let her pass. She favoured him with a long, searching stare and then a smile, saying, "Merci, monsieur."

"Come on, Gilly, for God's sake!" the man said in French. "We're late already."

They crossed to where a scarlet TR4 was parked, got in, and with a violent roar from the exhaust, the chunky man whipped the car dangerously fast into the main street and drove away out of sight at speed.

Girland approached the reception desk, setting down his suitcase.

"Mr Girland booking in," he said to the clerk. "Was that Mr Rosnold who just left? I believe I recognised him."

"That is correct, sir."

"He's not checking out?"

"Oh, no, sir. He is with us for another week."

Satisfied, Girland completed the usual form, went up to his room, unpacked his bag and changed into a sweatshirt and hipsters. As the time was only after 11.00 hrs, he decided to take a look at the country since he guessed Rosnold and Gillian could be out for the day.

As he left his room, an elderly chambermaid came along the corridor. Girland smiled, asking in his fluent German, "Is Mr Rosnold on this floor, do you know?"

"He's right there," the woman said, returning Girland's smile. She pointed to a door exactly opposite Girland's room. "But he's out now."

Girland thanked her and went on his way. He felt he had begun the assignment not only with a lot of luck, but well.

As he drove from the hotel, Labrey, sitting at a café near the hotel watched him leave. There was nothing Labrey could do about this. He would have to wait until Malik arrived, but at least, he knew where Girland was staying. The next move was to find out why he had come to Garmisch.

Girland returned to the hotel for lunch having driven as far as Wies where he visited what is considered by connoisseurs to be the most beautiful rococo church in Germany. Girland was not an admirer of this form of art, and after taking a hasty look around the massive, ornate interior, he decided to drive back slowly, savouring the magnificent scenery, the hills, the forests and the green of the rich spring meadows.

It was while he was driving along a narrow road bordered by wild flowers that he saw ahead of him a scarlet sports car, parked on the side of the verge. He slowed, seeing the hood was open and Gillian Sherman sitting in the passenger's seat. He slowed to a crawl, and as he approached, he saw Rosnold peering at the motor.

My lucky day, Girland thought and pulled up.

"Do you want any help?" he asked in French. Rosnold regarded him. He was a man in his middle forties, but in good trim with a well-built, muscular body. His eyes were a little too close-set and his mouth hard, but he was reasonably handsome. He smiled, a tight-lipped smile, then raised his hands helplessly.

"The damn thing just stopped. Do you know anything about cars?"

Girland slid out of the Mercedes and went over to the TR4. He purposely didn't look at Gillian.

"Try to start her," he said. "Let's hear what she sounds like."

Rosnold got under the driving wheel. The dynamo whirred, but the engine remained dead.

"All right for gas?"

"Three-quarters full."

"Then you could have dirt in the petrol feed. Got any tools?"

Rosnold found the tool wallet and handed it over. It took Girland ten minutes to get the engine restarted. He stepped back and smiled.

"There you are ... simple when you know how."

Rosnold said gratefully, "Thank you very much. You are most kind."

"Glad to be of help." Girland now looked at Gillian who gave him a wide, fascinating smile.

"I think you are wonderful," she said.

"If you will permit me, madame, I will return the compliment," Girland said. He gave her his long stare of admiration that had so often sent tingles up the spines of so many girls, then he returned to his car and drove off.

At the hotel he had a good lunch, then went up to his room, stripped off, put on a shortie dressing-gown and stretched out on the bed. Girland believed in rest when there was time to rest. Within a minute or so, he was asleep.

He woke a little before 18.00 hrs, took a shower, shaved and put on a midnight-blue suit, a white polo-neck sweater, black suede shoes. He surveyed himself in the full-length mirror. Satisfied, he pushed a small armchair up to the door, opened the door a crack and sat down to wait.

At 19.30 hrs he heard a door open and he became alert. Leaning forward, he peered through the crack to see Rosnold come out of his room, insert a key in the lock and turn it. Girland shoved the armchair away and moved out into the corridor. He too locked his door and turned to make for the elevator.

Rosnold recognised him and smiled.

"So we meet again," he said and offered his hand.

Girland shook hands.

"I didn't know you were staying here," he said. "No further trouble with your car?"

"No ... thanks to you. If you're not in a hurry, give me the pleasure of buying you a drink," Rosnold said. "I am most grateful to you."

"Not at all." Girland fell into step beside Rosnold. "I'm here for a short vacation. I've been cooped up in Paris too long and I felt the need to stretch my legs. Would you know of a good restaurant around here? I get bored with hotel meals all the time."

They reached the elevator and went down to the ground floor as Rosnold said, "You mean you are on your own? Come and dine with us. I would take it as a favour."

"But your wife ..." Girland let this hang.

Rosnold laughed.

"She's not my wife. We go around together. She'll be delighted. She's already told me she thinks you are dreamy."

Girland laughed.

"You certainly know how to pick them."

They went into the tiny bar and got the only corner table. Both ordered double Scotch on the rocks.

"I'm in the photographic racket," Rosnold volunteered as they waited for their drinks. "What's your racket?"

"I can't say I have one single racket," Girland said and grinned. "I work a number: agent for this and that. I work when I feel like it which isn't often. I guess I'm lucky. My old man left me some heavy money which I take care of."

Rosnold looked impressed. He eyed Girland's clothes which had been bought with Dorey's money from a top tailor in London.

"Some people have all the luck. I have to work for my living."

"You don't look as if you have to grumble."

"Oh, I get by."

As the drinks arrived, Gillian Sherman came into the bar. She was wearing a scarlet trousered cocktail suit of light nylon and wool with a gold link-chain around her slim waist. Girland thought she looked sensational. The two men got to their feet.

"This is Gilly ... Gillian Sherman." Rosnold blinked, then turned to Girland. "I'm sorry ... damn it I haven't introduced myself. Pierre Rosnold."

Girland was looking at Gilly.

"Mark Girland," he said and took the hand she offered. Her grip was cool and firm. Mischief and sex danced in her eyes and she surveyed him. "Miss Sherman, this brief encounter has made my vacation."

"What makes you think it is going to be brief?" Gilly asked as she sat down. "Pierre, a Cinzano bitter, please."

As Rosnold went to the bar, Girland said, "Two's company …"

She regarded him.

"Can't you do better than that?"

"I could."

They stared at each other. Girland gave her his intense look he had cultivated for just such an occasion. It was completely insincere, but it usually had a devastating effect on most women. Gilly reacted to it as he hoped she would. She leaned forward and smiled at him.

"Yes … I think you could," she murmured.

Rosnold joined them with the drink and set it before her. They talked. When Girland wished, he could be witty, amusing and often bawdy. Smoothly, he went into his act, and after a few minutes, he was holding the stage with Rosnold grinning appreciatively and Gilly doubled up with laughter.

It was while he was being his most entertaining that a tall, lean man came into the bar. He was about forty years of age with thick, flaxen hair taken straight back off a narrow forehead. His deeply tanned face was long and narrow and his alert eyes a washed-out blue. He wore a bottle-green velvet smoking jacket, a frilled white shirt, a green string tie and black trousers. Around his thick muscular left wrist was a heavy platinum chain. On his right wrist a platinum Omega watch. He had that confident, slightly arrogant air reserved for the immensely rich. He merely glanced at the three sitting at the corner table, then sat on a stool up at the bar.

"Good evening, Count von Goltz," the barman said, bowing. "What is your pleasure?"

"A glass of champagne ... my usual," the man said, and taking a heavy gold cigarette case from his pocket, he selected an oval-shaped cigarette which the barman moved forward to light.

"Phew!" Gilly breathed. "Some doll!"

Girland found her concentration in him had snapped. She was now studying the back of the blond man, her eyes calculating.

Rosnold touched her arm.

"Do you mind getting your eyes back on me, chérie?" he said, a slight rasp in his voice.

"Buy him for me, Pierre ... he's simply gorgeous." Gilly had deliberately raised her voice.

The blond man turned and regarded her. He smiled, an easy, pleasant smile.

"Your French tells me you are an American, mademoiselle, and I adore uninhibited Americans." He slid off his stool and gave a stiff little bow. Then looking at Rosnold, he said, "But I may be intruding, sir. If I am, I will take my drink into the lounge."

Both Rosnold and Girland got to their feet.

"Intruding? Of course not," Rosnold said. "Perhaps you would care to join us?"

"For a few minutes ... I would be delighted." Von Goltz pulled up a chair. "Count Hans von Goltz," and he bowed.

Rosnold made the introductions while Gilly continued to stare at von Goltz.

"You mean you are a real count?" she asked breathlessly. "I've never met a real count before!"

Von Goltz laughed.

"I am delighted to be the first." His eyes shifted to Girland. "And you? Are you also American?"

"That's right," Girland said. "I'm here just for a short vacation."

Von Goltz nodded.

"This is ideal country for a vacation." Sitting down, he began to talk about Garmisch and the surrounding district. Soon the conversation became general. When von Goltz had finished his glass of champagne, Rosnold asked him to have another, but von Goltz shook his head.

"Thank you, but I am afraid I must leave you. Please excuse me. I have a dinner date." He regarded Gilly. "If you have nothing better to do, perhaps you and your friends would care to visit my modest Schloss not far from here? It could interest you. I can offer you all kinds of amusements. There is a heated swimming pool, a lovely forest, twelve hundred acres of bridle paths and shooting – although at this season I can offer you only pigeons and rabbits. If any of you ride, I have horses. It would give me great pleasure to be your host."

Gilly clapped her hands, her eyes opening wide.

"That's marvellous! We would love to come!"

"My place is large and often lonely," von Goltz said and lifted his shoulders. "I live alone. I would welcome you all if you would care to stay for five or six days. I assure you you won't be bored. Would you all give me the honour of being your host?"

Gilly turned to Rosnold.

"Oh, do let's! It sounds absolutely dreamy!"

"It is very kind of you," Rosnold said. "If you are sure we won't be a burden, then we would happily accept your invitation."

Von Goltz looked smilingly at Girland.

"And you, sir?"

This really must be my lucky day, Girland was thinking. Now I will have the chance to talk to this girl alone.

"Thank you," he said. "As I told you, I am here on vacation. I would like nothing better. It is very kind of you."

Von Goltz shrugged.

"It will be my pleasure." He got to his feet. "I will send one of my servants here at midday tomorrow. He will direct you to the Schloss. It is only an hour's fast drive from Garmisch. You will arrive in time for lunch." He took Gilly's hand and brushed it lightly with his lips, then shook hands with Rosnold and Girland. "Until tomorrow ... good night," and with a pleased smile, he left the bar.

"What do you know!" Gilly said as soon as the count was out of hearing. "A real live count! And he has a castle! Gosh!"

Rosnold looked at Girland, a puzzled expression in his eyes.

"I didn't know Germans were quite so hospitable ... did you?"

Girland laughed.

"I very much doubt if you and I were on our own, we would have been invited. I think mademoiselle in her scarlet outfit caught the count's eye."

"Then you both should be very grateful to me," Gilly said, laughing. "Anyway, let's check out, Pierre. If we are going to stay at the castle for a week, there's no point in keeping our rooms on."

"Yes." Rosnold got to his feet. "And when we've checked out, we'll eat. I'm hungry."

The three went to the reception desk.

"We have been invited to stay with Count von Goltz,"

Rosnold explained to the clerk. "We will be checking out tomorrow morning. Will you have my bill ready?"

"Certainly, sir. You should have a very happy stay with the count," the clerk said, obviously impressed.

"That goes for me too," Girland said.

They went out into the courtyard where the cars were parked.

"Come in my car," Girland said. "There's more room."

Gilly slid into the front passenger's seat and Rosnold got in at the back.

"Where to?" Girland asked.

"Turn right as you leave the hotel. The restaurant is about eight kilometres from here. I'll direct you," Rosnold said.

Watched by Malik and Labrey who were sitting at the opposite café, Girland drove away from the hotel.

*   *   *

They made an odd-looking trio as they stood outside Garmisch's railway station. Vi with her long, blonde hair, her pale blue hipsters and red wool sweater looked absurdly small beside Malik who was wearing a short black leather coat and baggy black corduroy trousers, his silver coloured hair like a burnished steel helmet. Max Lintz in a coarsely-woven brown sweater and brown slacks with a brown woollen cap on his head stood on Vi's other side, his small, quick eyes examining the passers-by suspiciously and intently.

They had arrived only a few minutes ago. The time was just after 19.00 hrs. When Malik had reached Munich airport, he had gone to the Hertz Rental service and had hired a Volkswagen 1500. While he was waiting for the car to arrive, he had noticed a tall, white-haired man with a glass eye whom he had seen on the aircraft, standing near him. Malik merely glanced at him, and Lu Silk, not knowing who this giant was, gave him a steady stare from his one cold, hard eye and then looked away.

A big, black Mercedes pulled up and the driver waved to Silk who crossed the road and got into the car. As he was driven away, the Volkswagen arrived.

Malik told Lintz to get in at the back. Vi got in beside Malik, shrinking as far away from him as she could.

Malik had struck terror into Vi the moment she had seen him at Orly airport. He had come up to her, stared at her with his evil green eyes and had asked abruptly: "Mademoiselle Martin?"

She had nodded dumbly.

He had held out a huge, cruel-looking hand.

"Your passport."

With shaking hands, she had found her passport in her bag and had given it to him.

"Follow me," and he stalked into the airport.

They went together through the police barrier. For a brief moment Vi had been tempted to scream to the police officer that she was being kidnapped, but remembering Paul's warning, terror kept her silent.

In the reception lounge, Max Lintz had joined them. He had glanced at Vi without interest and then had drawn Malik aside. The two men had talked together in German, ignoring Vi who stood uneasily, shaking a little, while she waited.

On the aircraft, Malik had let her sit by herself while he and Lintz occupied the two seats behind her. All during the flight, they had talked softly in German while Vi had sat miserably wondering what was going to happen to her.

While waiting outside the railway station, she had screwed up her courage and asked Malik for her passport.

He turned and looked at her as if he was seeing her for the first time and didn't like what he was seeing.

"I keep it," he snapped and looked away.

"But it's mine!" Vi cried with a sudden desperate flash of courage. "You can't keep it. Give it to me!"

Lintz turned to stare at her as Malik said in his flat, dead voice, "I keep it."

Vi bit her lip and moved away. She felt trapped, and again terror went through her, leaving her cold and shaking.

"Here he is," Lintz said suddenly.

Labrey came hurrying up the street to join them.

"I lost my way," he said breathlessly, ignoring Vi. "I'm sorry I'm late."

Malik drew him aside.

"What has been happening?"

"Girland is at the Alpenhoff Hotel," Labrey said. "He has hired a Mercedes. Right now he is in the hotel."

"Is there a hotel near his?"

"Right opposite. I've booked us all in."

"Then we will go there now." Malik regarded Labrey. "You have done well."

Vi and Labrey got in the back of the Volkswagen and Malik and Lintz in the front. Vi put her hand on Labrey's and looked beseechingly at him, but he snatched his hand away. He knew Malik could see them in the driving mirror and he was scared of Malik.

It took only a few minutes to reach the Alpenhoff Hotel. The hotel opposite was more modest. Malik sent Lintz and Vi into the hotel and he and Labrey took a table on the sidewalk and ordered beer. From where they sat they could look directly into the Alpenhoff Hotel's courtyard.

They saw Count von Goltz leave in a silver-grey Rolls

121

Royce. He meant nothing to them. Then ten minutes later they saw Girland, Gilly and Rosnold come out and get into Girland's hired Mercedes and drive away.

"Who is the woman?" Malik asked.

"I haven't seen her before."

Malik brooded, then he said, "I want your girl's wristwatch."

Labrey gaped at him.

"Vi's watch?"

"Get it!" The snap in Malik's voice brought Labrey to his feet. He hurried into the hotel, up the stairs to Vi's bedroom where he found her sitting on the bed, her head in her hands. She looked up as he came in and jumped to her feet.

"He's taken my passport!" she said wildly. "You must get it back! Paul! I ..."

"Shut up! Give me your watch!"

She shrank back, staring at him.

"... My watch ... why?"

"Give it to me!" Labrey's thin face had that vicious expression that always frightened Vi. With shaking fingers she undid the gold-plated strap and handed him the watch.

Snatching it from her, Labrey left the room and ran down to the street.

"Here it is," he said, handing the watch to Malik.

Malik examined it and his short, thick nose wrinkled. "It isn't much but it will have to do. Wait here." He got to his feet and moved to the edge of the crowded sidewalk. He had to wait a few moments before there was a gap in the steady flow of traffic, then he crossed the street and walked into the Alpenhoff Hotel's lobby.

The reception clerk looked up from his work as Malik

came to rest at the desk. He stood up and inclined his head politely.

"Yes, sir?"

"A young lady left here a few minutes ago," Malik said in his fluent German. "She was wearing a red trouser outfit. As she got into her car, she dropped this." He held up the watch. "I wish to return it to her."

"Thank you, sir. I will give it to her with pleasure."

Malik regarded the clerk with a suggestive smile.

"I would like to give it to her myself. Who is she?"

"Miss Gillian Sherman. I believe she has gone out to dinner, but she will be back some time tonight."

"Then I will return the watch tomorrow. Would you tell her I have found it?"

"Certainly, but you should be here before ten o'clock tomorrow. Miss Sherman is leaving us." The clerk guessed this shabbily dressed giant was after a reward.

"If I miss her, do you know where she is going?"

"She will be staying at the Obermitten Schloss," the clerk told him. "Count von Goltz's estate."

"Then I will be back before ten o'clock." Malik walked across the lobby to the row of telephone kiosks. He put through a call to a Soviet agent in Munich. He learned the Obermitten Schloss was owned by Herman Radnitz. Malik knew all about Radnitz. He talked for some minutes to the agent, instructing him to call Kovski in Paris. The agent promised to call him back at the hotel as soon as he had made contact with Kovski. Malik left word with the hotel's telephone operator where he could be found and went into the hotel lounge to wait. An hour later, his Munich call came through. He listened to the information he was given, grunted his thanks and hung up.

6

It was after midnight when Girland returned to his hotel bedroom. It had been a good evening. The meal had been a little heavy, but excellent, and the restaurant, gay and amusing. Both Gillian and Rosnold had been good companions.

If it hadn't been for Dorey and his dreary assignment, Girland thought as he undressed, he would have thoroughly enjoyed the hours he had spent with these two, but mindful that he had to earn Sherman's ten thousand dollars, he tried to switch his mind to the best approach to get the three films from Gillian.

But full of good food and German wine, he couldn't be bothered, and decided to concentrate on the problem in the morning. Tomorrow, the three of them would be at the count's castle. There would certainly come an opportunity to talk to Gillian during their five days stay.

Taking a shower, and then getting into bed, he reached for a cigarette and lit it. Gillian had made an impression on him. She was beautiful, gay, amusing and sensual. He found it hard to believe she had taken part in the film he had seen. Thinking about her, Girland came to the conclusion that he dug for her.

Rosnold had also been amusing. Girland always kept an open mind about people. If this man made money by shooting pornographic films, this was no affair of his,

Girland told himself. What he did for a living didn't matter. This was Girland's philosophy. It was the people themselves that were important, not what they did.

While he was finishing his cigarette and thinking he would now sleep, the telephone bell at his side buzzed, startling him.

He picked up the receiver. "Yes?"

"It's me."

He recognised Gillian's husky voice and immediately he became alert.

"Hello … what do you want?"

"I'm lonely."

"Funny thing … I seem to be lonely too."

"Shall we be lonely together?"

"Then we wouldn't be lonely, would we? Two people together can't be lonely, can they?"

"Some can."

There was a long pause while Girland stared up at the ceiling, trying to make up his mind if this was a good or a bad move.

"I am in Room 462. It's at the end of your corridor," Gilly told him.

"Do you like it at the end of the corridor?"

Gilly giggled.

"This is an invitation, stupid, not a geography lesson."

Girland decided this invitation was unwise. Gilly was Rosnold's property. He didn't believe in poaching.

"It's too far," he said firmly. "Go to sleep," and he replaced the receiver.

He stubbed out his cigarette and relaxed back in bed. He didn't have to wait long. The door eased open and Gilly slid into his room, closing the door softly after her.

She had on a white robe to cover a shortie nightdress. Her slippers were pale-blue. She looked very attractive as she regarded him.

"Hello there," Girland said, smiling at her. "As lonely as all that?"

She came to the end of the bed and glared at him.

"You are a pig!" she exclaimed. "When you had my invitation, you should have come to me!"

"I told you to go to sleep," Girland reminded her. "But since you don't want to sleep, and since I don't want to sleep, you'd better get in here before you catch cold."

He flicked aside the blanket and sheet and shifted over to make room for her.

"If you imagine I intend to sleep with you now, you are making a great mistake. I came just to tell you that I think you're a pig!"

Girland flicked the blanket and sheet back into place.

"That has now been recorded ... I am a pig. Good night," and he reached for the bedside lamp and turned it off. The room was plunged into darkness.

"Put that light on!" Gilly said sharply. "How can I find my way out?"

"Fall over the furniture. I want to go to sleep," Girland said out of the darkness. "Good night ... I'll see you in the morning."

She groped her way around the bed as Girland, grinning in the darkness, once more flicked back the blanket and sheet. There was a pause, then he heard the rustle of her clothes as they dropped to the floor.

"I hate you," Gilly said, "but now I'm here, I will stay."

"I thought you might. It's a drag to walk all that way down that long corridor." Girland reached out, his hands sliding around her naked back, pulling her down on him.

126

He lay still with her resting on him. She began to unbutton his pyjama jacket. His hands moved down her back and clasped her firm buttocks. She gave a long ecstatic sigh and her mouth found his.

During his chequered career, Girland had known many women. The act of love to him was always a unique experience. Sometimes he was disappointed, sometimes he was satisfied, but this experience with Gilly was something he hadn't experienced before.

Later, they rested side by side, both breathless. Girland couldn't remember a more exciting and exhausting episode.

The moonlight came through the chinks in the shutters, making a pattern on the carpet. The sound of fast-moving cars came and went. Faintly he could hear swing music from the café opposite.

Gilly touched his chest. She sighed.

"I knew you had to be good, but I didn't imagine you could be that good."

"Sleep," Girland said. "No post-mortems."

She curled up against him, one long leg across his legs, her face close to his, her warm, scented breath fanning his neck.

They slept.

The sunlight coming through the shutters brought Girland awake. He screwed up his eyes and then opened them as he yawned. Gilly lay by his side, beautiful in her abandoned nakedness. She breathed gently, her shell-pink nipples bathed in a streak of sunlight.

Girland put his hand lightly on the apex of her thighs. She murmured something and turning to him, her eyes still closed, she slid her arms around him.

This drowsy passion was less violent than before but more gentle and more satisfying. Once she cried out, her body stiffening, but then she became relaxed again, her breath quick and irregular. Again they slept.

Later still, Girland woke, raised his head and looked at his strap watch. The time was twenty minutes after nine. He prodded Gilly gently.

"Time you went to your room," he said. "It's long after nine."

"Who cares?" Gilly said drowsily, stretching her lovely body. "Kiss me."

But Girland was alive to the risk. He had no idea what time Rosnold got up. He didn't want Rosnold to find Gilly's bedroom empty. He slid out of bed and went into the bathroom. Before turning on the shower, he called. "On your way. I'll see you downstairs in an hour."

When he had shaved and showered, he returned to the bedroom to find she had gone. He felt relaxed and fine. He ordered toast, marmalade and coffee and then dressed. He threw open the French windows and stood, breathing in the sharp May air, watching the movement of the people on the street below.

*　　*　　*

At the modest hotel opposite the Alpenhoff, Malik left his room, walked down the corridor to Labrey's room. He tapped and entered.

Vi, wearing bra and panties was making up her face before the small mirror. Labrey was putting on his shoes.

"Just bust in!" Vi said angrily, snatching up her wrap and struggling into it. "Haven't you any manners?"

Malik ignored her. He tossed her passport on the bed, then he signed to Labrey to follow him. Out in the passage, Malik said, "I have no further work for you two for the moment. You are to return to Paris." He took from a worn wallet several 100 DM bills and handed them to Labrey. "I am satisfied with your work. Lintz and I can now handle it. You are to report to Kovski. Tell him I am still following Girland. Tell him nothing else. Do you understand?"

Labrey nodded. He was relieved he could take Vi back to Paris. He had had a hell of a night with her.

"And she?" Labrey asked.

"Tell her she will work for us in the future. Give her some of that money. There is plenty for both of you," Malik said. "I thought I might use her here, but she is now no longer necessary. Get off quickly."

He left Labrey and went downstairs and joined Lintz who was sitting at a table outside the hotel.

"You've checked us out?" Malik asked as he sat down.

"Yes ... we're all ready to go."

"I've got rid of those two upstairs," Malik said. "They have served their purpose. Now, they will only be in the way."

"So what do we do now?" Lintz asked.

"The three of them will be going to the Obermitten Schloss some time this morning," Malik said, lighting a cigarette. "We follow them there. This is rather like a jigsaw puzzle, but now, the pieces are falling into place. I know now that this girl, Gillian Sherman is the daughter of the future President of the United States and that they are estranged. She is living with Pierre Rosnold, the man she is travelling with. He specialises in pornographic films. The girl is without morals and we can assume she has made a pornographic film. We know Sherman had a movie projector with him which he gave to Dorey who passed it on to Girland. I think it is obvious the girl is blackmailing her father. Now Radnitz's nephew appears on the scene. We know Radnitz and Sherman have a bargain. Radnitz will get a big contract from Sherman if Sherman becomes President. It would be in Radnitz's interest to stop the girl blackmailing her father. The girl, Rosnold and Girland have been invited to Radnitz's Schloss ... why? Knowing Radnitz, they are going there to get their throats cut."

"Do we care?" Lintz asked, looking at Malik.

"Yes. For reasons I will not discuss with you, we care," Malik said quietly.

Half an hour later, while the two men still sat watching the movement of the crowd as it passed along the narrow sidewalk, Labrey and Vi came from the hotel. Labrey was carrying a suitcase. He paused at Malik's side.

"We're on our way," he said. "If there is anything else ...?"

Malik shook his head.

"No ... you have been useful ... get off."

Vi stood away from Malik. She could scarcely believe she was leaving this silver-haired giant who so terrified her. With Labrey, she began to walk towards the railway station.

"Pretty girl," Lintz said, eyeing Vi's legs as she moved quickly along the street.

"A whore," Malik said indifferently, "but she will be useful."

"Yes." Lintz laughed, then seeing Malik was blank-faced and his eyes brooding, he cut off his laugh and remained silent.

A few minutes to midday, a black Mercedes turned into the Alpenhoff Hotel's driveway and pulled up outside the entrance. A short, thick-set man, wearing a green livery of cloth and leather, went into the hotel.

Malik became alert.

A few minutes later, the man came out followed by Gillian, Girland and Rosnold. Two porters carried their bags.

"They are on their way," Malik said. "Get our bags."

Lintz went into the hotel.

The short, thick-set man in the green livery was talking to Girland.

"If you will follow me in your car, sir, I will take you to the Schloss," he was saying. "It's about an hour's drive."

Gilly said to Rosnold, "I want to drive in the Merc. You follow us ... okay?"

"No!" Rosnold said curtly. "You are driving with me."

Overhearing this exchange, Girland went to his hired Mercedes and got in. Without waiting to see if Gilly was winning her argument, he started the engine and followed the black Mercedes out into the main street.

Seeing him leave, Gilly grimaced and shrugged. She climbed into the TR4.

Rosnold said, "Are you falling for that fellow?"

Gilly eyed him, then shook her head.

"If I'm going to fall for anyone, I'll fall for the count ... he has the money."

Rosnold got in the car and started the engine.

"I could get tired of you if you can't keep away from other men."

Gilly made a face at him.

"Would that be such a disaster?"

Rosnold scowled at her, then drove out into the main street and headed after Girland.

*　　*　　*

Count Hans von Goltz sat in a high-backed leather chair, facing Lu Silk who sat on a leather-covered settee.

The two men were in the baronial hall of the Obermitten Schloss: a vast room with wooden beams supporting the arched ceiling. The big picture window looked out onto the magnificent park with its close-cut lawns and gnarled trees. Beyond the set garden was the forest.

Count Hans von Goltz was Herman Radnitz's nephew.

Had it not been for Radnitz, von Goltz would now be serving a life sentence for murder and rape. When he was sixteen years of age and living with his parents on their estate near the Saxon Forest, east of Hamburg, he had come across an Austrian girl student on a hiking vacation. She had strayed onto the von Goltz land and she had asked him the way to the main highway to Hamburg. They were completely alone together, and von Goltz had made advances which were repulsed. Von Goltz was used to having his way. There was a struggle, and after the brutal rape, he had strangled the girl. Leaving her body half-concealed in the bracken he had returned home. He told his father what he had done. One of the gamekeepers who hated von Goltz had heard the girl's screams. He had arrived on the scene a few minutes after von Goltz had left. He had found von Goltz's watch by the body. It had been torn from von Goltz's wrist in the struggle.

It so happened that Herman Radnitz was staying at the Schloss, spending a few days with his sister, von Goltz's mother. Von Goltz's father, horrified at what his son had told him, went to Radnitz. Radnitz advised that they should do nothing. The girl's body would be discovered sooner or later. Both he and the parents would say von Goltz had been with them all during the afternoon.

But they were reckoning without the gamekeeper who raised the alarm. The police arrived and the gamekeeper gave them von Goltz's watch. Although the parents and

Radnitz confirmed the boy hadn't left the Schloss during the afternoon, he was arrested. His hands were badly scratched. White and trembling he had told the police he had been teasing one of the farm cats, but this explanation was not accepted.

Radnitz then talked to the gamekeeper. For an agreed sum of money, the gamekeeper told the police that he disliked young von Goltz and had fabricated the story about finding the watch by the girl's body. In fact, he had found the watch in another part of the estate and had intended to keep it. Radnitz then talked to the Chief of Police who had political ambitions. It was easy for Radnitz to arrange something advantageous and in return the Chief of Police dropped the murder charge. It had been a narrow escape and young von Goltz was grateful. A year later the von Goltz estate was wiped out by bombing and both von Goltz's parents killed. He had served in the German army and when he was released Radnitz sent for him. He offered him the stewardship of Radnitz's rich estate in Bavaria. He would receive an adequate income. He would handle the estate and generally put himself at Radnitz's disposal. Von Goltz jumped at this offer and for the past twenty-five years, he had acted as major-domo to one of the finest private estates in Germany. There were times when Radnitz would visit the estate, look around, satisfy himself that his nephew was doing a good job, have some hunting and then go away. There were times when von Goltz received an abrupt order to visit East Berlin where he met shabby men who handed him packages or letters which he delivered to Radnitz. Once he was ordered to go to Peking where he collected another mysterious package, but these courier jobs didn't often happen. Von Goltz was quite content to do what his uncle told him without question so long as he could remain at the Schloss to hunt, entertain his friends, have women who came from all parts of Europe for a short visit and indulge in his dream fantasy that this splendid Schloss and estate belonged to him.

The previous day, he had received written instructions from Radnitz, and for the first time since he had become Radnitz's steward, he had orders that made him flinch.

"It is necessary," Radnitz wrote, "to get these three films from this girl. You may use any method you may think fit, but she must be persuaded to give them to you. I am sending Lu Silk who will take care of the girl. You need have nothing to do with her disposal. Silk is a professional and is well paid and extremely efficient. But your job is to get the films. Until you have them, Silk is not to proceed with the next move."

"I've made it easy for you," von Goltz said as he sipped his champagne. "They will be arriving shortly. Once they are here, they won't be allowed to leave. I will get the films from the girl, then I will leave you to get rid of them all."

Silk nodded.

"Okay," he said. "I'll keep out of sight until you get the films." He thought for a long moment, then went on, "They'll be traced here. You realise that? The hotel will know they are coming. They just can't vanish into space."

Von Goltz shrugged.

"That's your affair. My affair is to get the films."

Silk smiled.

"It will be a mental exercise that will amuse me." He got to his feet. "I will keep out of sight. Be careful of Girland. The other two are harmless, but Girland is dangerous."

"My uncle has warned me."

Silk left the room. He walked slowly up the broad staircase to the second floor. A long walk down a corridor lined on either side by medieval battle weapons brought him to his suite which consisted of a bedroom and a vast sitting-room. He let himself into the suite, locked the door, then crossed to the window which overlooked the lower terrace and the main entrance. He sat down, lit a cigarette and stared blankly down the long, winding drive while he waited for the three to arrive.

*   *   *

The entrance to the Obermitten Schloss was imposing. The flint and stone walls surrounding the estate were twenty feet high with cruel-looking steel barbs mounted along the top of the wall. The tall wrought iron gates swung open as the black Mercedes slowed and then drove through. Girland followed. His sharp eyes noticed that on both gates was a heraldic shield of black metal. Inscribed in glittering gold leaf were the initials HR. This puzzled him. HR? he wondered. Why not H v G? As he followed the black Mercedes along the winding drive, bordered on either side by dense larch trees, he began to feel a little uneasy. He couldn't explain this uneasiness to himself, but the darkness of the overhanging trees, shutting out the sunlight and the barbed walls gave him a sudden feeling that he was driving into a trap. He told himself this was nonsense, but the feeling persisted.

He looked into his driving mirror and saw the TR4 was following behind. He drove after the black Mercedes for at least five kilometres, then suddenly the gloomy forest was gone and wide, immaculate lawns with ornamental fountains gushing water, banks of daffodils and tulips made a splendid scene against a backdrop of clear blue sky and lazily floating white clouds. Against this scene was the Schloss: an imposing, magnificent building with turrets, terraces ornamented with marble statues and an arched entrance through which two trucks could have easily driven side by side.

Gilly scrambled out of the TR4 and joined Girland as he got out of his car.

"Just look at this!" she exclaimed breathlessly. "It's the biggest and most perfect place I've ever seen!"

Rosnold joined them. He stood staring up at the building, shaking his head in wonderment.

The huge double wooden doors swung open and von Goltz came out onto the terrace. He waved to them, signalling to them to come up the three flights of marble steps that led to the main terrace.

"Welcome," he said, smiling.

While two liveried servants appeared to take their bags, the three walked up the steps and joined von Goltz.

"What a dreamy place!" Gilly said excitedly. "Do you really mean you live here all alone? There must be at least fifty rooms ..."

Von Goltz laughed. He was obviously pleased by her excitement.

"To be exact there are a hundred and fifty-five rooms," he told her. "It's absurd, of course ... an anachronism, but I love the place. I have lived here for twenty-five years. I couldn't bear to leave it."

Girland was looking at the terrace furniture. On each wrought iron chair was a tiny shield each bearing the initials HR. He glanced at von Goltz who was leading Gilly and Rosnold towards the entrance to the Schloss. He followed behind.

"Fritz will show you to your rooms," von Goltz said, waving to a short, fat man in livery. "You will wish to tidy up. Suppose we say lunch in half an hour?" he paused, then went on, "I have put you all close together on the first floor." He laughed. "It is easy to get lost in this place."

Twenty minutes later, Gilly came into Girland's enormous bedroom with its four-poster bed and its splendid view of the park and distant forest.

She was wearing a simple white dress and around her suntanned throat was a necklace of large blue beads.

"Isn't it marvellous?" she said, joining him at the open window. "Look at that bed ... it's made for love!"

Girland laughed.

"The one-track mind. Any bed is made for love ... it depends on who occupies it."

"I'm right next door." She lowered her voice as she continued, "I'll visit you tonight."

Girland lifted his eyebrows.

"I don't remember inviting you."

She laughed.

"You don't fool me, Casanova. You know you want me. You want me now ... anyway, I'm coming tonight."

"You have something there." Girland studied her. She was very desirable. "Where's Rosnold?"

"In his room. Let's go down. I'm starving."

They moved across the room together. At the door, Gilly paused, looked steadily at Girland, then said, "Kiss me."

As Girland took her in his arms, there came a tap on the door. They moved quickly apart, then Girland opened the door. Rosnold was standing in the corridor. He regarded Girland with a long, probing stare.

"I was wondering where you had got to," he said, shifting his stare to Gilly.

"Well, here we are. I was investigating his room ... look at it! It's marvellous, isn't it?" Gilly said innocently.

Rosnold glanced into the room and nodded.

"The whole place is fantastic. What it must cost to run!"

There was a gentle cough behind them and turning, they saw Fritz standing behind them.

"Lunch is served if you please," he said. "Will you come this way?"

The lunch was impeccable, served in an enormous high-ceilinged room that could cater for two hundred people. There were footmen in green and gold livery standing behind each chair. The meal began with white caviar, served with chilled vodka, followed by breasts of wild duck in a wine sauce with a 1949 Ausone claret. The dessert, served with a golden sauterne, was hot-house strawberries in a champagne sorbet.

During the meal, von Goltz chatted pleasantly, concentrating his attention on Gilly, but also including Girland and Rosnold.

Girland noticed the table silver all carried the initials HR and this again puzzled him.

As they moved from the big dining-hall into the lounge for coffee, Girland asked, "Who is HR?"

Von Goltz looked sharply at him, then smiled.

"You noticed the initials? This place doesn't actually belong to me but to my uncle."

"A perfect meal, Count," Rosnold said as he sank into an armchair. "I congratulate you. Your chef reaches the standards of my country and that is praise indeed."

"He is French," von Goltz said.

He sat on a satin-covered settee by Gilly's side. There was a pause while a footman served coffee and cognac.

When the footman had gone, von Goltz looked directly at Girland.

"You were curious about my uncle. I believe you have

met him."

Girland lit a cigarette. There was now an expression on von Goltz's face that he didn't like. Although he remained relaxed, he became mentally very alert.

"Have I?"

"Yes. He is Herman Radnitz."

Girland's smile remained polite and easy. So they had walked into a trap, he thought as he said, "Of course. Once we did some business together. How is he?"

"Very well."

"Will he be visiting you while we are here?"

"No." Von Goltz crossed one leg over the other. He sipped his coffee, staring thoughtfully at Girland. "I don't think we need waste any further time, Mr Girland. You realise now that you have walked into a trap?"

Girland put down his coffee cup and picked up his brandy glass.

"If Radnitz is behind your invitation, anything could happen," he said lightly.

Gilly was listening to this, her expression bewildered. "Can we share the joke, please?" she asked. "I don't understand."

"Of course," Girland said, stretching out his long legs. "The count's uncle is one of the richest and most evil men in the world. Had he not been so rich, he would be safely locked up in jail. His real name is Heinrich Kunzli. He made his fortune by supplying the Nazis and the Japs with soap, fertilisers and gunpowder. That seems harmless enough, doesn't it? But the Nazis and the Japs agreed to supply the raw materials for these products. The raw materials were the bones, hair, fat and teeth of the murdered millions from concentration camps. The count's nice uncle laid the foundation of his enormous fortune by turning into money the end-products of the dead bodies of Jews and other victims of the last war." Girland smiled at von Goltz. "That is correct, isn't it, Count?"

Von Goltz showed his teeth in a mirthless grin.

"Yes ... near enough, but it is old history now." He regarded Girland, his eyes glittering. "You are an interfering, useless man, Girland. This time you will cease to interfere."

Girland sipped his brandy and nodded his approval.

"I've heard all that before ... I can't say it ages me."

Gilly exclaimed, "For God's sake ... just what is this?"

"Let me explain," von Goltz said quietly. "You are blackmailing your father. You have three films which you are threatening to send to his opposition party unless he withdraws from the election. I want these films." He stared at her, his eyes suddenly cold. "I intend to have them."

Gilly started to her feet. Blood rushed to her face and then drained away. Her eyes sparkled with anger.

"You're not getting them!" she cried. "Pierre! Let's get out of here! Come on ... don't sit there like a dummy! Let's go!"

Rosnold was studying von Goltz who toyed with his brandy glass, relaxed and smiling. His smile sent a chill up Rosnold's spine. He looked at Gilly.

"Sit down and shut up!" he said sharply. "Can't you see, you fool, we're caught!"

"Caught? He can't stop us ... I'm going if you're not!" Gilly rushed across the room, jerked open the door and dashed into the vast hall. She ran to the high entrance doors which she found locked. She tugged at the bolts while six heavily-built men in the count's livery watched her with mask-like faces. The bolts were immovable and with a cry of rage, she spun around, rushed back into the lounge, darted past the three men who watched her and dashed out onto the terrace.

Below, on the driveway, was the scarlet TR4. With a gasp of relief, she started across the terrace to run down the three long flights of marble steps. Then she stopped short. Two huge black alsatian dogs stood at the bottom of the steps and snarled at her. Their white fangs sent a cold shudder of fear through her. She stared down at the dogs, hypnotised with horror. Crouching low and still snarling, the dogs began to climb slowly up the steps towards her. Gilly's nerve broke. Whirling around, she ran back into the lounge.

"Those dogs ..." she began breathlessly then stopped as von Goltz laughed.

"Why don't you sit down?" he asked. "You can't get away. Yes ... those dogs ... they will tear you to pieces if you are stupid enough to challenge them. Where are the films?"

Gilly faced him, white and scared, but her eyes still flashed with rage.

"You're not getting them!" She turned to Rosnold. "Do something! Tell him ... don't just sit there! Do something!"

"I warned you." Rosnold was pale and uneasy. "I'm not going through with this. I've had enough of it."

Girland listened to all this. For a moment he was forgotten. The action now was between Gilly and Rosnold with von Goltz as an interested spectator.

"He's not having them!" Gilly cried, beating her fists together. "He can't force us to give them to him! He can't!"

"But you are mistaken," von Goltz said, his voice sounded bored. "When I want something, I always get it.

Do you want me to give you a demonstration of my persuasive powers?"

"Go to hell!" Gilly shouted at him, her eyes flashing. "You're not having those films! If you don't let us leave I'll – I'll call the police."

Von Goltz regarded her as he would regard a difficult child.

"You are still very young and still very stupid. How do you call the police?"

Gilly turned desperately to Girland.

"Aren't you going to do something?" she demanded, going to him and standing over him. "Do you call yourself a man ... just sitting there? Get me out of here!"

"The Count holds the four aces," Girland said quietly. "I don't bet against such odds. Give him the films."

She turned away from him in disgust.

"You're not having them!" she said, spinning around to confront von Goltz. "Understand? You're not having them!"

Von Goltz waved her away. He looked now at Rosnold and his eyes were glittering with suppressed fury.

"You realise, of course, I have ways to persuade you both?" he said. "Why let us have any unpleasantness? Where are the films?"

Rosnold licked his dry lips.

"If you tell him, I'll kill you!" Gilly screamed furiously. "He can't force us ..."

Von Goltz came out of his chair very quickly. He hit Gilly across her face with the back of his hand with cruel violence. She catapulted across the room, smashed into a small occasional table and sprawled on the floor, flat on her back.

Girland looked down at his hands. This wasn't the time

to go into action. He knew for certain that if he made a move the big room would be filled with von Goltz's servants.

Rosnold half started to his feet, staring at Gilly as she lay, sobbing, her hands holding her aching face.

"I apologise," von Goltz said quietly. "I didn't want any unpleasantness, but this stupid girl doesn't seem to realise the situation." He paused then looked at Rosnold. "Where are the films?"

"In my bank at Paris," Rosnold said.

"You stinking coward!" Gilly cried, scrambling to her feet. "How could you tell him!" She started across the room towards Rosnold, but Girland was out of his chair and intercepted her. He ducked her flying fist and pulled her against him.

"Play it cool," he said softly. "Don't get so excited. You can't win all the time."

She stared for a long moment at him, then she threw off his hands and walked unsteadily to a chair away from him and sat down.

Girland returned to his chair and sat on the arm. He took out his pack of cigarettes, shook out a cigarette and lit it.

Von Goltz said, "You will write a letter to your bank, Mr Rosnold, telling them to give the films to the bearer of the letter." He pointed to a desk standing in a corner of the room. "You will find paper and envelopes there. When my messenger returns from Paris with the films, you three will be free to leave here."

Rosnold hesitated, then got up and went to the desk. He wrote rapidly, addressed the envelope and then gave the letter to von Goltz to read.

"Excellent. Thank you for your co-operation." Von Goltz got to his feet. "In two days you will be free to go. In the meantime, please amuse yourselves. I would not advise you to leave the terrace. The dogs are extremely dangerous. However, there is a swimming pool at the back terrace you may use. There is a billiards room. Make yourselves at home. I will see you all again for dinner. If there is anything you want, please ask Fritz."

He left them, carrying the letter, his smile showing his satisfaction.

Girland got to his feet.

"After that lunch, I think I need a nap," he said. He looked at Gilly. "Maybe we'll meet in a couple of hours at the swimming pool."

He walked into the hall where the servants stood watching him. He stared at them and they stared woodenly back, then whistling softly under his breath, he climbed the stairs to his room.

*   *   *

At 16.00 hrs Girland came from his room wearing a pair of swimming trunks and carrying a towel over his shoulder. Fritz was waiting in the corridor. He bowed to Girland and led the way down to the swimming pool.

The heated pool was at the rear of the Schloss and so positioned that it caught the afternoon sun. It was some twenty metres long with a high dive board and around it were set out tables, lounging chairs, li-los and sun umbrellas.

Girland dived in and swam the length, then turning on his back, he floated in the warm, blue water, staring up at the sunlit sky. He hadn't been in the water for more than a few minutes when Gilly appeared, wearing a white bikini. She took a racing dive into the water and swam past him with a showy, fast crawl.

Girland watched her as she spun, around, kicked off

against the side of the bath and made for the other end. She swam well, almost professionally. When she reached the far end, she hoisted herself out of the pool and sat on the edge, her feet in the water.

With a slow, lazy crawl stroke, Girland swam towards her. Reaching her, he trod water, looking up at her.

"Got over your temper?" he asked with a smile.

"Oh, stop it!" she said sharply. "It isn't funny! What is going to happen to us?"

He caught hold of her ankles and hauled her into the water. She splashed down beside him. His hand supported her, keeping her head above water.

"We're being watched," he told her. "There is a man on the second floor right window watching us."

Gilly swam around the pool and then rejoined Girland.

"Who is it?"

"Your guess is as good as mine. Let's sunbathe. Keep your voice down and don't get excited. Remember you are being watched."

They hauled themselves out of the pool and stretched out on li-los.

Fat Fritz appeared with cigarettes and a lighter. He asked what they would like to drink. Gilly shook her head, but they took cigarettes. Girland waved Fritz away. When he had left the terrace, Girland said, "I hope you now realise the spot we're in?"

Gilly lit the cigarette and half-turned on her side to look at him.

"You puzzle me ... just where do you come in on all this?"

"Your father hired me to get your films." Girland spoke softly. He was lying on his back, staring up at the blue sky. "What defeats me is how a girl like you could have made

145

such films."

"Are you telling me you are working for my father?" Gilly half sat up, then controlling herself, she relaxed back on the li-lo.

"That's what I'm telling you. I work for anyone who pays me," Girland said. "I don't like your father. I don't like you. This is a job ... simple as that."

"You don't like *me*?" Gilly glared at him. "You didn't dislike me last night!"

"When a woman walks into my bedroom and throws herself at me – especially when she is as well put together as you are – I take what she offers," Girland said. "But that doesn't mean I like her or think anything of her."

"Oh! Just why don't you like me?"

"Because you are a blackmailer." Girland released smoke down his nostrils, eyeing the burning end of his cigarette. "Blackmailers are never my kind of people."

Gilly lay still, her hands on her breasts. Her face had lost colour and her mouth was now a thin, hard line.

"All right ... I'm a blackmailer. How else could I stop my father becoming President? I don't give a damn about myself ... I never have, but I am determined he isn't going to be President. I used the only weapon I had to stop him."

Girland turned his head to study her.

"Tell me why you want to stop him?"

"I'll tell you ... because he is unfit for high office. Because he is weak, vain and stupid. Because he and my mother only think of themselves and seeing themselves with power."

"That's your point of view ... I'm not saying you are wrong. You're working with Rosnold, aren't you? This Ban War organisation gives you a kick, doesn't it?"

"And why shouldn't it?"

"It's the old story, Gilly ... people like to be big fishes in a small pond. If Rosnold and his organisation wasn't so interested in you – and they are interested because you can stop a man from becoming a President – you wouldn't be making this trouble. Isn't it because this organisation is making you an important person, you are blackmailing your father?"

"All right ... if you like to think that ... I don't care! There are many reasons. Anyway, he made a mess of my life ... now, I'm going to make a mess of his!"

"Are you sure he made a mess of your life?" Girland asked. "Are you sure you're blaming him instead of blaming yourself?"

"Don't feed me that stuff!" Gilly said fiercely. "Neither of my parents wanted me ... they did everything they knew how to get rid of me. So now I'm in the position to give them something really to be ashamed of. I don't expect you to believe this ... and I don't care, but I hated making those films. Pierre promised me once they were made, my father couldn't become President ... so I made them."

"Oh, come on!" Girland said impatiently. "I don't believe it. Why don't you face facts, Gilly? You are an immoral slut. You have let this weak-kneed organisation go to your head. You are glorifying in being someone important because you are in the position to stop a man becoming President of the United States. If it wasn't for Rosnold and this organisation, you wouldn't give a damn if your father became President or not."

"God! I hate you!" Gilly said. "Everything you've said is not true!" She sat up and leaning over him, she went on fiercely, "This count can have the films! Why should I care! When I get back to Paris I will make other films! My father is not going to be President!"

"When you get back to Paris?" Girland stubbed out his cigarette. "What makes you think you are going back to Paris?"

She stared at him, her eyes opening wide.

"Of course, I'm going back to Paris! What do you mean?"

"You can't be this dumb," Girland said as he stared at a floating cloud. "When von Goltz gets the films, he will make sure none of us leave here and neither you nor Rosnold ever make another stag film."

Gilly lay for a long moment, frowning, then her eyes opened wide with shock.

"But he can't do that! How can he? He said once he had the films, we were free to go. As soon as I get back to Paris, I will make more films!"

"The trick with this is you don't return to Paris."

Gilly began to say something, then paused. She lost colour as she stared at Girland.

"You can't mean ...?"

"Of course. When the films arrive, your nice, handsome count will get rid of us permanently." Girland lifted his head and looked across the wide, immaculate lawns to the distant, dense forest. "There are plenty of convenient places out there for a triple burial."

"You mean he will murder us?" Gilly sat up. "I don't believe it!"

"If he is anything like his charming uncle ... and I'm sure he is ... he won't hesitate to wipe us out as you wouldn't hesitate to swot a fly."

"But you can't kill three people ... just like that." Her voice was husky and her eyes alarmed. "I don't believe it! The hotel knows we are here. When – if – we are reported missing, there will be an inquiry. The police ... he can't ...

he wouldn't dare."

"I saw something interesting from my bedroom window before I came down here," Girland said, closing his eyes against the sun. "One of von Goltz's servants drove off in your TR4. Another of his servants drove off in my car. At a guess, the TR4 will be found at the Munich car park. My car could be found anywhere. Yes, of course the police will come here, but von Goltz is important in this district. He will tell them we were here for the night and then left for Paris. He has no idea what could have happened to us. You can't expect the police to dig up every metre of this enormous estate in the hope of finding our bodies, can you?"

Gilly shivered.

"I just don't believe it ... you're trying to frighten me because you hate me!"

Girland shrugged.

"I don't hate you, Gilly. I just think you're a mixed-up kid and I must admit I'm so bored with mixed-up kids. Listen: the messenger will arrive in Paris around 22.00 hrs tonight. He will pick up the films tomorrow morning and catch the 14.00 hrs flight back to Munich. He should be here with the films around 18.00 hrs. So we have from now until 18.00 hrs tomorrow to dream up a way to get out of here alive."

Gilly said, "You really believe this man will kill all three of us when he gets the films?"

Girland got to his feet and draped his towel over his shoulders. He smiled down at her.

"Wouldn't you if you were in his place?" he said and walked across the terrace and up to his room.

Gilly looked across the wide sweep of lawn. At the edge of the forest she saw the two black alsatian dogs, their heads resting on their paws, staring towards her.

With a sudden sick feeling of fear, she scrambled to her feet, snatched up her towel and ran after Girland.

From the upper window, Lu Silk touched off the ash of his cigarette and stood up. He regarded the distant dogs, then crossed the room to where a .22 target rifle, equipped with a telescopic sight, lay on the table. He picked up the weapon and balanced it in his capable, killer's hands. He liked the feel of it. Carrying it to the open window, he aimed the rifle at one of the alsatian dogs. The cross hair line of the telescopic sight centred on the dog's head. Silk adjusted the sight slightly, bringing the dog sharply into focus, then satisfied, he lowered the rifle and put it against the wall.

There came a tap on the door and von Goltz came in.

"The two cars have gone," he said as he closed the door. "Are you satisfied that it will be safe to get rid of them here?"

"Yes ... where else?" Silk sat down. He put a cigarette between his thin lips. "Where can we bury them?"

"There is a rubbish tip in the forest that is permanently smouldering and white-hot," von Goltz said. "They can be thrown there. The morning's refuse will cover them."

"You can trust your servants?" Von Goltz hesitated.

"Yes ... I think so."

Silk stared at him. His one eye was probing.

"That's up to you ... if you are sure, then it's settled."

Von Goltz took a turn around the room.

"How will you do it?" he asked finally.

"A little target practice ... it could be amusing." Silk went over to the .22 rifle and picked it up. "This is a fine weapon. Send them out onto the lawn and I'll pick them off like rabbits."

Von Goltz flinched.

"Be careful of Girland."

Silk grinned.

"I'll take him first," he said and put the rifle down on the table.

* * *

As Girland entered his bedroom, he knew instinctively that someone had been there while he had been in the pool. This he expected. After closing and locking the door, he went to his suitcase and tossed out its contents on the bed. He regarded the bottom of the empty case with a nod of satisfaction. Whoever had searched the case had been an amateur. He pressed the tiny spring, hidden under the lining of the case. The bottom of the case clicked open, revealing a tray in which were his professional weapons. They consisted of a Walther automatic pistol with a magazine capacity of 8 rounds, a razor-sharp double bladed stabbing knife and a tear gas bomb. When Girland travelled on business, he travelled well equipped.

Satisfied none of his weapons had been discovered, he shut the false lid and replaced his clothes in the suitcase.

Then he stripped off his wet bathing trunks, towelled himself and put on a wrap. He went out onto the balcony and sat in the basket-chair from which he could overlook the immaculate lawn. He sat there for some time, smoking and thinking and watching the two alsatian dogs as they prowled around the rough grass on the edge of the lawn and the forest.

When the light began to fail and the air became chilly, he returned to his room. He took a hot shower and then dressed for dinner. It was while he was knotting his tie that his door slammed open and Gilly rushed in: her eyes wide with fright, her face white.

"You've got to stop him!" she shrilled, reaching Girland and grabbing his arm. "He's trying to get away!"

Girland's mind immediately reacted.

"Where is he?"

"He's climbing from his balcony down to the terrace!"

Girland moved swiftly out onto the balcony. He was in time to see Rosnold drop onto the terrace below. Rosnold held a medieval battle-axe which he had taken from the corridor wall. As Girland spotted him, Rosnold started across the terrace.

"Rosnold! Come back!" Girland shouted.

Gilly joined him on the balcony. She too screamed after Rosnold who paid no attention.

"Come back!" Girland bawled, but Rosnold kept on. He took the steps leading from the terrace to the lawn two at the time and then disappeared into the heavy shadows. They could hear the thud of his feet as he began to run across the lawn.

Suddenly, from the roof of the Schloss, a searchlight snapped on ... a blinding ribbon of light. It picked up Rosnold as he raced across the lawn, giving him a grotesque shadow five times his own height that fled before him. From out of the darkness an alsatian dog appeared, moving fast and silently. Rosnold stopped short, turned and faced the dog as it sprang at him. The axe, the blade glittering in the beam of the searchlight, swung and there was a crunching sound as the blade crushed the dog's head. As Rosnold began to run again, the second dog appeared. It sprang at him, his fangs bared. Rosnold swayed away, and the dog went past him, rebounded and sprang again. Rosnold was ready, and again the axe swung. The dog gave a yelp of pain and rolled over, snapping at its damaged leg.

Gilly choked back a scream and hid her face. Girland leaned over the balcony rail, watching.

Still holding the blood-stained axe, Rosnold darted off to the left, and for a brief moment the finger of the searchlight lost him, then it picked him up again as he continued on his way, running very fast, across the lawn. He was within four or five metres of the entrance to the dense forest when there came a snap of gunfire.

Lu Silk, standing on his balcony, immediately above Girland's balcony, felt a surge of satisfaction as he lowered the .22 rifle. Rosnold had jumped high in the air with the reaction of a shot rabbit as the tiny bullet had slammed into the back of his head and through his brain. Considering how fast Rosnold had been running and also considering the poor light, Silk decided that this was the best shot he had made for a long time. He patted the butt of the gun to convey his appreciation.

"They've killed him!" Gilly moaned, staring across the lawn at Rosnold's still body, lighted by the searchlight. "I told him! I warned him, but he panicked! He wouldn't listen to me!"

Girland paid no attention to her. He moved swiftly back into his room, ran to his suitcase and threw out the contents on the bed. He opened the false bottom and took the automatic pistol from its resting place and shoved it into his hip pocket. Then he threw the contents of the suitcase back in and slammed the lid.

Gilly came into the room from the balcony, white faced and shaking.

"Get hold of yourself!" Girland snapped. "This is the crunch! Where's your passport?"

She stared at him, dazed.

"Passport?"

"Where is it?"

"In my room."

"Get it ... hurry!"

"They've killed him!" She began to wring her hands.

Girland grabbed hold of her and shook her.

"Get your passport!"

Crying, she ran blindly from the room and into her bedroom. Girland went after her. He shut his door and as he entered her room, she was fumbling at her bag. He snatched it from her, opened it, assured himself the passport was in the bag, then grabbing her arm, he rushed her out into the corridor.

"Don't make a sound!"

Moving silently, he pushed her up the stairs to the upper floor, paused to look along the long corridor and then pushed her up the next flight of stairs. As they were stumbling up the stairs, Girland heard the thudding of feet as von Goltz's servants came running up the lower stairs.

Girland reached the third landing which was in darkness. He paused to lean over the banisters and peered down the well. He watched three liveried men come down the corridor on the first floor landing and charge into his bedroom.

He waited long enough to see one of the servants come out and rush to the head of the staircase and shout, "He's not there!"

Then as a bell began to clang, Girland took Gilly's arm and led her silently further down the dark corridor.

7

A Volkswagen 1500 stood by the roadside near the imposing entrance to the Obermitten Schloss. A silver-haired giant, wearing a shabby suit was working on the engine. Another nondescript-looking man sat on the grass bank, smoking.

Occasionally a car roared by on its way to Munich. No driver stopped to ask if he could help. The dwindling rays of the evening sun came through the trees, making patterns on the roof of the car.

Malik loosened a sparking-plug for the fifth time. He wanted to give the appearance of a breakdown. Although he was sure he wasn't being watched, he was taking no chances.

As he began to tighten the sparking-plug, the wrought iron gates of the Schloss swung open and a scarlet TR4 came cautiously onto the main road.

Malik straightened up and looked at the car as it gathered speed, driving past him. He knew the car belonged to Rosnold, but Rosnold was not at the wheel. The car was being driven by a thick-set, blond man wearing an ill-fitting business suit.

Malik's mind worked swiftly. He made an instant decision. He slammed down the cover over the engine and said, "Go after him!"

Lintz was already on his feet. He slid under the driving wheel.

"What about you?" he asked as he started the engine.

"Never mind about me!" Malik snapped. "Go after him! Don't lose him! When you know where he has gone, report to Skoll."

Lintz nodded, engaged gear and drove off after the fast disappearing TR4 which was heading for Munich.

Malik moved into the surrounding forest. He sat down on the dry, dusty ground, using a shrub as a shelter. Five minutes later a Mercedes car which he recognised as the one Girland had been driving, came through the open gates and turned left. A man Malik didn't recognise, who was wearing the same kind of shabby suit as the driver of the TR4, was at the wheel. The Mercedes headed towards Garmisch.

Malik rubbed his jaw as he thought. It now looked as if he had guessed right. Girland, the girl and Rosnold had walked into a trap. Getting rid of their cars was the first step towards getting rid of them.

There was nothing he could do about this for the moment. He would have to wait until it was dark. With the patience of a trained agent, he relaxed against a tree and waited.

Two hours later, it was dark enough for him to make a move. He got to his feet and silently left the forest. He began to walk around the high wall surrounding the Schloss.

Some four hundred metres from the entrance gates, he paused and looked up at the towering concrete and flint wall. He studied the spikes set in the top of the wall. From his shabby jacket he produced a length of thin, nylon cord. At one end of the cord was a rubber-covered hook. He tossed the hook towards the spikes. The second throw succeeded. The hook settled silently around one of the spikes and held firm. Malik glanced from left to right.

Satisfied there was no traffic, he caught hold of the cord, braced his feet against the wall and walked up, his strong hands hauling him effortlessly to the top. Here, he paused, and surveyed the dense forest below. He unhooked the cord, manoeuvred himself around the sharp spikes and then let himself drop onto the dry, mossy ground on the other side of the wall.

He paused to coil the cord to a convenient size to fit his pocket, then drew from a shoulder holster a Mauser 7.63 pistol, fitted with a silencer.

Moving like a shadow, he walked through the forest until he eventually reached the clearing between the forest and the wide, closely cut lawn.

The moon was behind the clouds, and Malik could just see the distant lights from the Schloss. He squatted against a tree, nursing his gun and waited. An hour dragged by, then suddenly things began to happen.

From a first floor window, Malik saw a man appear on the balcony. There was a brief glimpse of a woman, but the man threw her violently back into the room. The man climbed over the balcony rail, hung for a moment, then dropped heavily to the terrace below. He recovered his balance and darted down the steps to the lawn.

Malik stood up, watching.

Suddenly a bright beam from a searchlight flashed on from the roof of the Schloss and picked up the running man.

Malik watched the brief, deadly battle between the man and the two alsatian dogs. He watched the man start to run fast towards him, then he heard the crack of a sporting rifle and saw the man drop.

Malik moved silently back into the darkness of the forest. He remained there, motionless while two men came across the lawn and carried the lifeless body back to the Schloss. Lu Silk and von Goltz stood on the lighted terrace, looking towards the forest. Von Goltz held a microphone in his hand.

Speaking slowly and clearly, his voice picked up on the speakers in the forest and along the walls of the Schloss, he was saying, "You cannot leave the grounds. Don't go near the walls. A lethal electric current has been turned on. Please come back. Mr Rosnold is not badly hurt. He is recovering. Please come back."

Listening to this, Silk moved impatiently.

"Are you sure they can't get out?"

Von Goltz switched off the microphone.

"Impossible ... no one can get out now. The walls and the gates are lethal, but it could take time to find them. If I had more dogs, I'd flush them quickly, but without dogs ..."

"Can't you get more?"

Von Goltz shook his head.

"Those two dogs that swine killed were trained to hunt men. The dogs belonging to my neighbours are sporting dogs. Besides, there would be questions asked. When it is light, we will have a hunt in the forest. It could be amusing. I am satisfied these two can't leave the estate." He paused, then went on, "But if they attempt to climb the walls ..." He switched on the microphone and again repeated his warning that the walls were lethal.

In the shadows, Malik listened and grimaced.

Girland, standing on the third floor balcony overlooking the terrace, concealed in the darkness, also listened and grinned. He moved back into the vast dark room that seemed to be full of heavy furniture. He closed the windows.

"It's working," he said, joining Gilly. "They think we are in the grounds as I thought they would." He produced a tiny, powerful electric torch and swung the beam around the room. "This looks big enough for a railway station." He took her hand and led her down the aisle between the furniture until they reached a door. Gently, he opened it, listened, then threw the beam of his torch into what appeared to be a small retiring room. "Let's settle here," he said. "It looks less grand."

Breathing fast and shaking, Gilly followed him into the room and he closed the door. His torch directed her to a dust covered settee.

"Sit down."

They sat side by side.

"What are we going to do?" she asked. He could feel she was trembling. "If they find us ... they'll murder us, won't they?"

"They have to find us first." Girland leaned close to her. "They won't start looking for us until tomorrow when it is light. With any luck, they will search the forest. While they are out there, I'll go down and find a telephone. I'll call the US Army in Munich. They'll arrive in force and we'll walk out. There is nothing to worry about. You'll just have to make up your mind to forget about having dinner and wait until tomorrow morning."

"Call the army? Are you crazy?" Gilly tried to see Girland's face in the dim light. "Why should they bother with us? You must call the police!"

"No ... the US Army," Girland said. "Because, my pet, you happen to be the daughter of the future President. When I tell them you have been kidnapped, the whole US Army stationed in Germany, plus tanks and aircraft will come rushing to your rescue."

"No!" Gilly said fiercely. "I'll never trade on my father's rotten reputation!"

Girland sighed.

"Are you sure?"

"Yes ... I'll never ..."

"All right ... all right ... don't get so worked up. You have made your point. So you don't want the US Army to rescue you?"

"No!"

"A pity ... it could have been fun to have lots of tanks bashing down the gates and fat Generals rushing up the drive. All right, then here's what you do. Go downstairs and find the count. When you find him, tell him you won't accept your father's favours and would he please cut your throat."

Gilly sat for some moments, speechless.

"Oh, I hate you!" she exploded, thumping her fists on her knees. "You are horrible ... you don't understand!"

"I'm afraid I do ... the trouble with you is you have grown up physically too fast and mentally too slow. We're wasting time. Are you sure you don't want the army to rescue you?"

"I would rather die!"

"You probably could. All right ... fair enough. Girls with principles bore me. They're always a nuisance. Well then, I'll run along. You stay right here until they find you. I don't need the US Army to get me out of here. Since you are stuck with your principles, I leave you with them. So long ... thanks for the bed session which was wonderful." As he got to his feet, Gilly grabbed his arm.

"You're not leaving me?"

"Yes ... reluctantly, but I am leaving you. I believe in looking after myself. Beautiful dumb girls with political ideas are always a hindrance. Give me ten minutes, then either sit tight or go down and talk to the count ... who knows, he might just possibly marry you, but I suspect he will slit your pretty throat."

"How I hate you!" Gilly exploded. "How can you think of leaving me?"

"Don't get worked up, baby," Girland said soothingly. "It's your choice. There is another possible alternative." He sat down again. "You and I could make a deal. I could get you out of here without calling in the US Army, but we would have to come to an agreement first."

"What do you mean? What agreement?"

"You would have to promise me to leave your father alone in the future. You would also have to promise me that you will give up running around with this half-baked Ban War organisation and you would have to promise me never ever again to make a stag film."

She drew in a long, quivering breath.

"So you really are working for my father!"

"No ... I'm working for myself. I am a mercenary. I took your father's assignment for the money. I don't give a damn about him, but when I take an assignment, I deliver. You either give me your promise or I'm going to walk out on you. I can always take care of myself. Frankly, Gilly, I don't give a damn about you or your father. If you think you can take care of yourself and get to Paris and make more blue films, you go ahead and do it."

"This is blackmail," Gilly said, suddenly calm.

"So what? Is it against any rules to blackmail a blackmailer?" Girland asked. "There is time ... think it over. I'm going to admire the view."

He crossed the room, opened the French windows and moved silently out onto the balcony.

The long searching finger of the searchlight was still probing the forest. He could see a group of men, wearing the count's livery moving across the lawn towards the forest. He again heard the metallic voice of the count over the speakers repeating his warning that the walls were lethal.

He remained out in the darkness watching the activity below, glad now there were no dogs. However, there were plenty of men and he made a rough count ... possibly twenty-six or even thirty. It was difficult to count them as they kept disappearing and reappearing in the light of the searchlight. Finally, he decided he had given Gilly long enough to make a decision. If he didn't get her promise – he wondered what her promise was worth – he wouldn't leave her, but he hoped his bluff had made an impression. He stepped back into the dark room, closing the French windows behind him.

"Well? Do we say goodbye?" he asked.

He could just see her, sitting on the settee. She was looking towards him.

"If I promise, what guarantee do I have that you will get me out of here?"

"What guarantee have I that you will keep your promise?" Girland came and sat by her side.

"When I make a promise, I keep it. All right ... I'm a slut ... I'm no good ... I have no morals ... I'm an alley cat ... but I do keep a promise."

Listening to her strained, fierce whispering, Girland was impressed.

"If you don't keep this promise," he said, "then there is nothing in this world that can make any sense for you. You'd be better off dead."

162

"Oh, stop nagging!" Gilly said angrily. "When I make a promise I keep it! How many more times do I have to tell you! But can you get me out of here alive?"

"I can't swear to it, Gilly. Out there are some thirty armed men. We have an electrified wall. We have an expert marksman armed with a sporting rifle who knows how to shoot fast. We have the count who won't let us go easily. A lot of odds but I will try. Without you, I could get out, but with you, the operation slows down, and it will be much more difficult, but not impossible. I'll get you out of this if I possibly can. You haven't any alternative. Without me, you would never get out. With me you stand a good chance. If we fail ... it won't matter about your promise. They have killed Rosnold ... they have to kill us. It's as simple as that. You will have to do exactly what I tell you. You must try to keep your nerve. This isn't going to be easy ... but it is possible."

"All right ... when you get me out of here, I will give you my promise and I will keep it."

"I'll accept that. Now let's do a little exploring. We have the night before us. Let's find a bed."

"You don't mean you can even think of sleeping?"

"Why not? We have a long time ahead of us before we leave."

"Why can't we go tonight?"

"I want those films. When I hand them over to your old man he is going to pay me ten thousand dollars. I need that money. So we stick around here until the films arrive. Then – and not before then – we'll leave."

"You're crazy!" Gilly's voice shot up a note. "You'll never get them! They'll never let us walk out of here!"

"Just relax, Gilly. You must have confidence in me. I'm not leaving here without those films. I've told you you have a good chance of getting out of here. Leave this to me. Now come on ... I want to find a bed."

*   *   *

Seeing the line of men coming towards the forest and towards where he was standing, Malik moved silently further into the undergrowth. Each advancing man was carrying a powerful flashlight as well as a shotgun and the beams of light stabbed into the darkness.

This didn't worry Malik. He would never have ordered a search to be made in this forest in such darkness. To find any fugitive unless he betrayed his presence by noise was impossible in such surroundings.

He looked up at the tree against which he was standing. He could just make out a lower branch within his reach. He stepped back, jumped and caught hold of the branch. Easily, he hauled himself up, and in a moment he was climbing the tree with the silent agility of a cat. He paused when he was halfway up the tree, straddled a branch and set his back against the trunk.

He waited, looking down, seeing the stabbing beams of the advancing flashlights, hearing the crashing of undergrowth as the men moved forward into the forest. They passed below him and went on. He lifted his shoulders in contempt.

The search went on for an hour, then the leader of the party finally decided they were wasting time and energy. The men came back through the undergrowth. By now the time was 20.30 hrs and Malik, watching the men as they walked slowly across the lawn back to the Schloss, decided they were thinking of their dinner. He watched them disappear into a side entrance. A heavily-built man, wearing the count's livery, walked up the steps to where two men were sitting, waiting.

"Well?" Von Goltz snapped.

"It is impossible and useless, Excellency," the man said. He was Sandeuer, von Goltz's trusted major-domo: a man of some forty years of age with a tanned, fleshy face and shifty, cunning eyes. "We can't hope to find them in this darkness. Tomorrow ... yes, but not now."

"Are you sure you will find them tomorrow?"

Sandeuer bowed.

"It will take a little time, Excellency, but they can't get away. Besides, by tomorrow, they will be hungry and thirsty."

Von Goltz waved him away. When he had gone, Silk finished his whisky and soda and regarded von Goltz.

"You satisfied?"

Von Goltz shrugged.

"I have to be. They could be anywhere in the forest. Although my men know every centimetre of the ground, Sandeuer is right. In the darkness, it is impossible. When there is light, with the number of men I have, we will find them. Girland is unarmed. I had his clothes and his suitcase searched while he was in the pool. He has no weapons. So ... it is a matter of time."

One of the footmen came out onto the terrace to announce that dinner was served.

In the vast dining-hall, the two men sat down to a well presented and cooked dinner. Von Goltz, who liked his food, noticed that Silk was merely toying with what was put before him, his thin, hatchet-shaped face expressionless, his one eye showing no animation.

"Have some more of this sole," von Goltz said. "I think it is excellent."

"No ... I've had enough." Silk pushed his plate away.

"It doesn't please you?"

Silk shrugged impatiently.

"Fine ... fine ..." he snapped. "I'm not hungry."

This remark irritated von Goltz who would have liked a second helping of the sole cooked with diced lobster tails and in a heavy cream sauce. Angrily, he motioned the footman to change courses.

"You are worrying about something?" he asked, staring at Silk.

"We will discuss it later," Silk said as the second course of baby lamb was set on the table.

Now it was von Goltz's turn to be worried. He had been warned by Radnitz about Girland. For the moment, Girland had slipped through his fingers. Girland was out in the open with some two hundred acres of forest land to hide in. Although von Goltz was sure Girland could not get out of the estate and he was not armed, he might take a long time to corner.

The switch that operated the current to the walls was in the lodge at the entrance gates. In the morning when the tradesmen arrived it would be necessary to cut the current to let them in. Girland might discover this and make a break over the wall. But could he discover this?

Suddenly losing his appetite, von Goltz left his meal half finished. He turned to the footman standing behind his chair and told him to get Sandeuer immediately.

Silk too had lost interest in the food and again pushed his plate away.

"What is it?" he asked, eyeing von Goltz.

"Girland ..." von Goltz got to his feet. "I don't like the idea of him being out there ... free. I know he can't get away, but ..."

The door opened and Sandeuer entered.

"What is happening at the lodge?" von Goltz demanded.

"It is all right, Excellency," Sandeuer said, bowing. "I have three armed men there. They will remain on duty all night."

Von Goltz relaxed.

"Good. Make sure they are continually on the alert."

"Yes, Excellency," and Sandeuer withdrew.

"A little cheese perhaps?" von Goltz said, sitting again at the table. The reassuring news had restored his appetite. He was now sorry to have dismissed the meat course.

"Not for me," Silk said impatiently and walked across the room to the open French windows. He moved out onto the terrace and stared across the moonlit lawn to the dark forest.

Von Goltz regarded the basket of cheeses, hesitated, then with a muttered curse, shoved back his chair and joined Silk on the terrace. He disliked Silk. This tall, cold American had no manners and his ruthless face unnerved von Goltz. He knew this man had the ear of his uncle. He was sure a critical report from him would mean he would be turned out of the Schloss. He had no illusions about his uncle. When a man was found wanting by Radnitz he was either dismissed or worse, he disappeared.

"What is it now?" he demanded.

"I'm trying to put myself in Girland's place," Silk said. He lit a cigarette. "I'm beginning to wonder if we are being fooled. We are assuming because Rosnold tried to escape, Girland and the girl also made a break. We are assuming that while Rosnold killed the dogs, Girland and the girl got down onto the terrace and made for the forest to the right instead of crossing the lawn as Rosnold did. But suppose they didn't? Suppose instead, they went upstairs? If I had been in his place, I think that is what I would have done. There are many rooms in this place ... many places to hide in." He looked at von Goltz. "We could spend days hunting for them in the forest while all the time they could be right here."

Von Goltz stiffened.

"Surely Girland wouldn't be so stupid as to let himself be trapped here?" he said. "He had the chance to get into the open ... surely he would have taken it?"

"Would he? He isn't to know you have no other dogs. I think he could still be here ... with the girl."

"We'll soon see. I'll have the place searched."

"Even if they are not here," Silk said, "it will give your men something to do. Yes ... have the place searched." He returned to the dining-room. "I think I will now have a little cheese," and he sat down at the table.

Von Goltz sent for Sandeuer.

This was the second time Sandeuer's dinner had been interrupted. When he received the message that the count wanted to see him immediately, he threw down his knife and fork with an oath. The five senior servants who were eating with him, concealed grins. Sandeuer was not popular. The chef said he would keep Sandeuer's dinner hot and Sandeuer, still cursing, hurried upstairs to the dining-room.

"It is possible," von Goltz said as he cut a large wedge of cheese, "that the fugitives have not escaped into the forest. They could be still here. Take men and search every room."

Sandeuer thought of his unfinished dinner.

"Yes, your Excellency," he said bowing, "but may I suggest that as the top floors have no lighting and are crowded with furniture, a thorough search by flashlight would be difficult. If I may suggest the search could be much more thorough tomorrow morning when the shutters can be opened and every inch of the rooms upstairs examined."

Von Goltz looked at Silk who shrugged.

"Very well, but post a man at the head of every landing. He is to remain there and keep watch. As soon as it is daylight, the search is to begin."

Sandeuer bowed and returned to his dinner after giving instructions for the landings to be guarded.

*　　*　　*

Girland decided it would be safer to go up to the fifth floor of the Schloss. He had checked the number of floors – eight in all – when he had arrived. By going up to the fifth floor, he had three more floors in which to manoeuvre should the need arise.

Holding Gilly's hand and using his flashlight sparingly, he led her down the long corridor to the stair head. The thick carpet deadened their footfalls. All he could hear was Gilly's fast breathing, and very faintly, the clatter of dishes as dinner was being served below. He thought regretfully of the food he was missing.

They went silently up the long flight of stairs, paused for a moment, then continued on up another flight of stairs. This landing was in complete darkness. No light from the ground floor reflected up the stair well as far as this.

Girland paused to listen. He heard nothing and moving away from the stair head, he turned on the flashlight. A white drugget covered the carpet. There was a slight smell of damp and must. He led Gilly down the corridor. On either side were doors. He paused at the fifth door. Easing the door open, he peered into darkness, listened, then turned on his flashlight.

The room was large. Standing against one of the walls was a four-poster bed. The windows were heavily shuttered. Girland moved into the room and Gilly followed him. He closed the door.

"This will do," he said. "Come on ... let's go to bed."

"I do wish we could get out of this awful place," Gilly said as he led her over to the bed.

"You will tomorrow. Hungry?"

He felt her shudder in the darkness.

"No."

"Lucky you ... I am. Well, Dumas once said the man who sleeps, dines. So let's go to sleep."

"I couldn't ... I'm too scared."

Girland stretched out on the bed and pulled her down beside him.

"It's a pity you didn't think of being scared when you made those films," he said, sliding his arm around her. "Couldn't you see you were sticking your neck out when you started this blackmail idea with your father ... he's a toughie if ever there was one."

"I'd do it again!" Gilly said but without much conviction in her voice ... She pulled away from him. "And stop nagging!"

"Sorry ... I was forgetting you are a mature, well balanced woman."

"Oh, shut up! You madden me! Listen ... suppose we go down to the count and tell him he can have the films and I promise not to make any more if he will let us go ... suppose we do that?"

"A marvellous idea." Girland laughed. "He will have the films by tomorrow anyway. Why should he trust you? Why should he let you go?"

"But you are going to trust me."

"Yes, but I have to … he doesn't. Go to sleep," and Girland moved away from her, made himself comfortable and shut his eyes. In a few moments, he was in a light sleep while Gilly stared fearfully towards the invisible ceiling. After a while, she began to think back on her past life. Although still hating her father and mother, she was now regretting what she had done. She reluctantly admitted that Girland was right. The Ban War was a weak-kneed organisation. She had only joined because she knew it would enrage her father. She thought of Rosnold, now realising with a sense of shock that she wasn't sorry that she wouldn't ever see him again. He had been her evil influence, she told herself. Without his persuasion and his flattery, she would never have made those awful films. She felt hot blood of shame run through her. How could she have done it? Of course that massive dose of LSD had made the films seem fun at the time. If Rosnold hadn't given her the LSD she wouldn't have done what she had done. She was now sure of that.

If she ever got out of this mess, she told herself, she would begin a new life. To hell with her father! If he became President, then the American voters got what they deserved! She would have to leave Paris. The Ban War mob would never leave her alone if she stayed. She would go to London. She had a cousin there working at the American Embassy. He might help her find a job. She listened to Girland's gentle breathing and she envied him. She remembered their night of lovemaking. He was the sort of man she would like to hook up with, but she knew that was hopeless. He was a loner … he had called himself a mercenary. He wouldn't consider having her around with him for long.

She thought of him with envy. Men had all the advantages.

Then suddenly she stiffened and her heart began to race. Had she heard voices? She half sat up and Girland's hand closed over hers. He had become instantly awake.

"What is it?"

"I thought I heard voices."

"Stay here."

Although she couldn't see him in the darkness, she felt the bed ease as he slid silently off it.

"Don't leave me!" she whispered urgently.

"Wait there!" His voice was the barest sound but there was enough snap in it to force her to remain on the bed.

Girland moved to the door and listened. Hearing nothing, he put his hand on the ornate gilt door handle and gently levered it down, then he edged open the door.

A faint glow of light met his eyes. It came from the head of the stairs.

Then he heard a man, speaking in German, say, "Are you all right down there, Rainer?"

A voice said something that Girland couldn't catch.

"Me?" the first voice said. "How can I be all right ... sitting on these stairs for the rest of the night?" There was a laugh, then silence.

Girland edged open the door and peered down the corridor. He saw a heavily-built man, wearing the count's livery, sitting on the top stair at the head of the staircase. Between his knees, his hands clasped around the barrel, was a shotgun.

The sight of this man startled Girland. Why was he there? Girland asked himself.

Could it be that the count suspected that Gilly and he hadn't escaped into the forest but had remained hidden in the Schloss?

It seemed to Girland this must be the explanation why this man was guarding the staircase. But if the count thought they were still here, why hadn't a search been organised? Girland considered this and then realised the difficulties of searching such a vast place in darkness. It looked now that the count had sealed off the landings and was waiting for daylight.

Girland closed the door softly and returned to the bed. He sat beside Gilly and told her what he had seen and what he thought would happen in the morning.

"You mean they know we are here?" Gilly gasped fearfully.

"They can't know, but I think they suspect we could be here. Now just relax. We have a lot of space to manoeuvre in. If you do exactly what I tell you, they won't find us. But if you lose your nerve, they will find us."

"What are we going to do?"

"We'll wait. We have lots of time."

Gilly started to speak, then stopped. There was a long pause while Girland stretched out on the bed.

"Relax and let me think," he said.

Gilly tried to relax, but it was impossible. She willed herself to remain still. Time crawled by.

She became aware suddenly that Girland's breathing had changed slightly and she realised he was asleep. She lay by his side, miserable and envying him his complete indifference to the danger that was crowding in on them.

Then she heard a sound that made her stiffen: a faint, but distinctive sound of snoring coming from the corridor.

Girland said softly, "Hear that? The guard has gone to sleep."

"Oh ... I thought you were asleep."

"So I was, but I sleep lightly." She let him slide off the bed.

He went to the door, eased it open and peered along the corridor. He saw the guard, sitting on the top stair, his head resting against the banister rail. From him was coming the gentle snoring sound.

Girland closed the door and switched on his torch. He crossed to the high windows.

"Come on, Gilly, we have work to do."

She scrambled off the bed and joined him.

"Catch hold of these curtains and hold them together."

When she had a firm grip on the heavy, velvet curtains, he took hold of the thick green and gold rope that opened and shut the curtains and threw his weight on it.

For a moment it held, then came away from its fastening and dropped to the floor.

He did the same with the other side of the curtain. Then he moved to the second window.

Within a few minutes, he had eight metre lengths of heavy curtain cord on the floor: these he began to knot together.

"What are you doing?" Gilly asked as she held the flashlight so he could see.

"Confusing the situation," Girland said. "When you're in a spot, confusion is your best friend."

He opened one of the windows, unlatched the heavy wooden shutter and eased it back.

Then he stepped out onto the balcony and looked down. There were no lights showing from any of the windows below. The light of the moon lit the vast expanse of lawn, and the distant forest was only visited by the outline of the tree tops.

He began to lower the knotted rope down the side of the outer wall, keeping the rope well clear of any window or balcony. The end of the rope finally dangled above the balcony on the second floor.

"We want two more curtain ropes," he said. "Wait here. I'll get them."

"Let me come with you."

"Do what I tell you!" Girland said curtly and moved to the door. He opened it, watched the sleeping guard for several moments, then slid out into the corridor. He entered the room next door.

A few minutes later, he returned as silently as he had gone with two more lengths of cord. These he knotted to the end of the cord dangling from the window and then continued to lower the cord which now just reached the ground. He tied his end to the balcony rail and moved back into the room.

"It might fool them," he said. "Even if it doesn't, it will gain us time."

"Can't we use those ropes? We could get out of here!"

Girland shook his head.

"I could, but you couldn't, so we don't go that way."

She caught hold of his hand.

"Once we get free, I promise I'll leave my father alone. I won't ever bother him again ... I promise."

"All right, but first we have to get out of here. Now, let's get moving. Take your shoes off. I want to look at the other rooms. This one is too small."

They both took off their shoes, then Girland opened the door and watched the sleeping guard, then led Gilly out into the corridor.

Silently, they moved away from the head of the stairs, down the long dark corridor to the far end. At the end of the corridor, double, ornate doors faced them.

Girland briefly used his flashlight. "Wait," he said softly.

He went forward, listened against the door, turned a handle and eased the door open. He listened again, then put on the flashlight.

The beam scarcely penetrated the vastness of the room which appeared to be a banqueting hall. For a brief moment, Girland was startled to see shadowy figures lining the walls.

A further probe of his light showed him this was a vast hall full of armour, fitted to stands and the walls covered with medieval weapons.

He wasn't to know that in this room was one of the finest collections of Italian, German and English armour that Herman Radnitz had collected from all parts of Europe.

He returned to where Gilly was waiting.

"We have lots of company," he said. "Come on in. This looks as good a hiding-place as we can hope for."

As she entered, Girland gently closed the door.

The guard at the head of the staircase continued to sleep.

*　　*　　*

From his tree top perch, Malik watched Girland come out onto the fifth floor balcony and lower the knotted curtain cord until it reached the second storey.

He watched him lean over the balcony rail, look down and then move back out of sight. Malik guessed he was getting more cord.

The bright light of the moon lit up the face of the Schloss and Malik found it unnecessary to use his night glasses. He eased his broad back against the trunk of the tree and waited.

Girland returned and added two more lengths to the cord and then fastened his end to the balcony rail.

So they were going to make a break, Malik thought. The climb down would be dangerous: with the girl, doubly dangerous. He continued to watch with interest.

But nothing further happened.

The wooden shutter remained half open; the balcony remained deserted.

A half hour crawled by. Malik then decided that this length of rope was a red herring.

He nodded his approval. He had come up against Girland several times and each time, his admiration for the way Girland handled a situation increased.

So, after all, Girland had decided to remain in this enormous Schloss, but to give those who were hunting for him the hint that he and the girl had escaped into the forest. Malik approved of this plan.

He remained astride the thick branch of the tree for another half hour.

All the lights of the Schloss had long gone out. It would be when the sun came up behind the hills that the hunt would begin.

He considered what he should do. Girland was in there on his own.

The girl would be more a hindrance than a help.

Malik remembered that moment when Girland could have had him shot, but instead, to Malik's amazement, Girland had handed him back his gun, saying to the girl who had wanted to shoot him: "Don't get worked up, baby.

* see *Have This One On Me*, by James Hadley Chase

He and I just happen to be on the wrong side of the Curtain. Both of us are professionals ... working in the same dirty racket. There comes a time when we can forget the little stinkers at the top who pull strings ..."*

Malik remembered this incident vividly. This, he knew, was something he would never have said to a man he had in a hopeless trap.

Girland's words had made a tremendous impression on him. *There comes a time when we can forget the little stinkers at the top who pull the strings ...*

Malik thought of Kovski, plotting at his desk, his shabby suit food-stained, his energy and thoughts bent only on mischief ... a little stinker ... yes ... Girland was right.

But Girland, with this girl, was now trapped in the Schloss. Malik decided this was the moment to pay off his debt.

He remembered a phrase that was drummed into him when he was learning English: *One good turn deserves another*. How often had he repeated this phrase while the gloomy, red-nosed teacher had corrected his pronunciation. This phrase was a cliché, but clichés often were true.

He swung himself down from branch to branch until he dropped onto the moss and the dead leaves of the forest.

Then he moved off, silently, like a big, dangerous cat, skirting the forest until he reached the edge of the lawn. Here, he paused and studied the face of the Schloss.

His next move would be dangerous. Although there were no lights showing, he wasn't to know if someone was watching. His thick fingers closed over the butt of the Mauser pistol.

He drew the gun from its holster, then moving swiftly, he raced across the lawn and into the sheltering shadows of the Schloss.

He paused at the foot of the steps leading to the terrace and waited. He heard nothing: no one shouted: no one raised an alarm.

Satisfied, he climbed the steps and reached the terrace, then made his way quickly past the tables and the folded sun umbrellas to where the curtain cord was hanging.

He put his gun back into its holster and took hold of the cord. He pulled at it with his immense strength. It held. He pulled again: again it held.

Placing his feet against the face of the wall, he began a slow, steady walk up to the first balcony.

Here he paused, gripping the balcony rail with his left hand, his feet wedged into the back of one of the dragon heads that decorated the wall.

He listened and waited, then moved to the second balcony.

The climb to him was easy. He was a man of tremendous strength and fitness. He was also nerveless. The thought that the rope might break and he would crash to his death meant nothing to him.

By stages, he finally reached the fifth floor balcony, swung his legs over the rail and paused before the open shutter and the open window.

He had come up silently, but he knew Girland had a highly developed sense of hearing. To walk into the black darkness of the room would be asking for trouble.

He remained on the balcony, listening, but heard nothing. Girland could be near, out of sight, thinking one of the count's men had come up by way of the rope.

"Girland ... this is Malik," Malik said in his guttural English. He pitched his voice softly. "Girland ... this is Malik."

He waited. There was silence. Slowly, he moved forward, turning on his powerful flashlight. The white beam lit up some of the room.

He stood in the doorway, sending the beam of the flashlight to the four-poster bed, then around the room. Satisfied the room was empty, he entered.

He stood in the middle of the room. So Girland had arranged his red herring and had left the room. Malik nodded his approval. But where was he?

Malik went silently to the door, eased it open and immediately stiffened when he saw a faint, flickering light in the corridor. He looked out, watched, the sleeping guard for several moments, then moved silently into the corridor.

Doors faced him. Somewhere on this floor, Malik reasoned, Girland, with the girl, was hiding.

He hesitated. He had to be careful not to wake the sleeping guard.

He couldn't go from room to room, calling Girland. It would be unwise to enter any room without first alerting Girland who he was.

Finally, he decided to get as far away as he could from the sleeping guard and find himself a hiding-place.

He moved silently down the corridor until he reached the double doors at the far end.

He looked back, assured himself the guard was still sleeping, then eased open the door.

Here he paused, listened, heard nothing, then he stepped into the darkness of a vast banqueting hall.

8

The sun came up from behind the hills, first lighting the tops of the trees and then the turrets of the Schloss.

Hans von Goltz had been shaved by his valet, and was now putting on a leather hunting jacket as he paced the vast floor of his bedroom. The shutters had been thrown open. The May air was sharp but pleasant. The first rays of the sun came into the room, lighting the tapestries on the walls and the splendid Persian carpet on the floor.

His breakfast, on a wheel trolley, stood in a ribbon of sun. Silver covers kept the two dishes warm. Von Goltz considered breakfast the most important meal of the day. As soon as he had shrugged himself into his coat, he went to the trolley and lifted first one and then the other silver cover: scrambled eggs, done lightly with plenty of butter, surrounded a fillet of smoked haddock. Lambs' kidneys with creamed potatoes in the second dish also pleased his eyes. He helped himself liberally and began his breakfast. While he was enjoying his kidneys – the fish demolished – there came a tap on the door. Frowning, he called to come in.

Sandeuer bowed his way through the doorway.

"Your Excellency ... excuse me, please, but you should know there is a rope hanging from the fifth floor balcony."

Von Goltz shovelled another kidney, covered with potato into his mouth as he glared at Sandeuer. When he could finally speak, he said, "A rope? What do you mean?"

"A curtain rope … if your Excellency would look … you will see for yourself."

Von Goltz got to his feet, snatching up a square of buttered toast and moved onto the balcony. He bit into the toast as he regarded the knotted curtain cord. Then he returned to the room.

"Have you told Mr Silk?"

"No, your Excellency."

"Then tell him. Ask him to come here immediately."

Sandeuer bowed and withdrew.

Realising his breakfast was about to be interrupted, von Goltz proceeded to bolt down the remaining kidneys. Then buttering more toast, he spread the toast heavily with cherry jam and began to eat so rapidly he nearly choked himself. He was still munching when his door swung open and Lu Silk came in.

Silk was wearing a black shirt, black cotton trousers and black shoes. Von Goltz thought he looked like the impersonation of death. Silk paused in the doorway and stared at von Goltz with his cold, single eye.

"You have seen the rope?" von Goltz asked, gulping down the last of his toast.

"Oh, sure." Silk moved into the room. "I saw it half an hour ago."

"So you were right! They were here last night, and now they have escaped into the forest."

"Could be." Silk sat down and lit a cigarette. "It's light enough now. You had better get the search organised."

Von Goltz moved around the room. His hurried breakfast had given him indigestion. He wished he hadn't eaten so quickly.

"As they are in the forest, there is no point wasting time searching here."

"Go ahead," Silk said, letting smoke drift down his nostrils.

Von Goltz stalked to the door, opened it and found Sandeuer waiting in the corridor.

"Begin the search," he snapped. "They are somewhere in the forest. Bring them back here. I don't have to tell you what to do. Find them!"

"Yes, Excellency," Sandeuer said, but as he was about to leave, Silk appeared behind von Goltz.

"Wait." Silk put his hand on von Goltz's arm and drew him back into the room. He shut the door. "I have an idea. I want you to go with your men. I want everyone out of here and into the forest."

Von Goltz stared at him.

"What do you mean?"

Silk stubbed out his cigarette in the ashtray on the breakfast trolley.

"I think they are still here," he said. "The quickest way to find them is for them to think everyone here is searching the forest."

"Still here?"

"Why not?" There was an impatient note in Silk's voice. "Have you looked at the rope? A man could get down it, but no woman could. As we have already sealed off each landing, they will be up on the fifth floor. I take it there is no other way down from the fifth floor except by the main staircase."

"That's right."

"So they are still up there."

Von Goltz rubbed the back of his neck while he thought. "Then I will send my men to the fifth floor and we will get them," he said finally. "Why waste time searching the forest?"

Silk smiled: it was an evil smile that made von Goltz flinch.

"We won't be wasting time ... we will be taking precautions."

"I'm afraid I don't understand. If you are so sure they are on the fifth floor, then with enough men, we will have them."

"And then what?"

The two men looked at each other.

"I still don't understand," von Goltz said after a long pause.

"You have a staff of forty men ... perhaps more?"

"The staff is thirty-eight men and five women. What does that have to do with it?"

"I want all your men out in the forest," Silk said, lighting another cigarette. "The women must also leave. I want this place completely evacuated." His thin, cruel face was expressionless. "What the eye doesn't see, a Judge doesn't know about."

"What do you intend to do?"

"Get rid of Girland. We will keep the girl until the films arrive. It is possible Rosnold was lying. When we have the films, then I will get rid of her."

"You mean you intend to stay here completely on your own?" von Goltz asked uneasily. "Is that wise? We have been warned about Girland."

Silk sneered.

"He is unarmed. I can handle him. All I have to do, once the place is evacuated, is to wait, out of sight. He needs two things: food and the possible use of a telephone. For both these, he has to come down the stairs. I'll be waiting for him."

"Are you sure you shouldn't have two or three of my men with you?"

Silk studied von Goltz.

"Can you guarantee none of them would talk later?"

Von Goltz saw the point.

"I see ... there is always that risk. When you have got rid of Girland ... what do you do with him?"

"With the body?" Silk smiled. "I have been studying the interesting plan of the Schloss you lent me. Is there water in the well in the rear courtyard?"

"Yes ... it is never used, but there is quite a lot of water."

"Well then, what better place? The girl, once we have the films, can go the same way."

Von Goltz felt a little sick. He wiped his sweating hands on his handkerchief. The casual, cold-blooded way this man talked shocked him.

"Well ... I – I will leave it to you."

"How will you get rid of your women staff?"

Von Goltz hesitated while he thought.

"There is a fair on at Garmisch. I'll send them there."

Silk nodded.

"Then let's get started. First, get rid of the women."

Von Goltz looked at his watch.

"It's not eight-thirty yet. This will take time. You know what women are."

"Then get your men into the forest. Let's start something!" Silk said impatiently.

Von Goltz went into the corridor to give his orders to Sandeuer.

When Sandeuer heard that the women staff were to be taken to the fair at Garmisch, he gaped at von Goltz.

"But your lunch, Excellency ... the rooms are yet to be done."

Von Goltz waved him away.

"Never mind! I want everyone out of here. Arrange it and arrange it quickly!"

Because he knew better than to argue with his master, Sandeuer hurried away to obey his orders.

There was an uproar and a great deal of heated talk from the chef and his staff when they were told that they were to go out into the forest to look for two missing guests. The chef, an enormously fat Frenchman, declared he was not going. He was about to prepare a complicated sauce and he had no intention of going out all day into the forest. It was only when Sandeuer threatened to call the count that the chef was finally convinced that for once his culinary expertise had to take second place. Red faced and furious, he tore off his white uniform and put on his green livery. Half an hour later the exodus from the Schloss began. From every quarter, men left and headed across the vast expanse of lawn towards the distant acres of the forest.

Later, five women, chattering and excited, left by car, heading towards Garmisch.

Sandeuer, sweating but triumphant, came up to the first floor to report that his master's orders had been obeyed.

Von Goltz told him to wait in the corridor. He shut the door and regarded Silk who was lighting yet another cigarette.

"Then I leave you?" he said.

"Yes. I have the place to myself?"

"All the staff has gone. You are quite sure you don't want me to stay with you?" von Goltz asked reluctantly.

Silk smiled mirthlessly.

"Do you want to?"

"I want this operation to be a success."

"I didn't ask you that." Silk lowered his voice and stared at von Goltz with his hard, single eye. "Do you want to be an accessory to murder?"

Von Goltz lost colour. His mind went back into the past and the terror he had known until Radnitz had saved him. He turned and walked out of the room and joined Sandeuer.

"Let us see what the men are doing," he snapped and strode down the stairs to the terrace.

Silk got silently to his feet. He went swiftly to his room. From his suitcase he took a 7.65 mm Luger automatic. He checked the magazine, then holding it in his hand, he went silently down the corridor, down the stairs and into the main living-room. He opened the double door leading into the hall and to the foot of the staircase.

Silently, he moved a chair so that he could just see the stairs when he sat in the chair without being seen himself. He guessed he would have a long wait, but he was used to waiting.

Sooner or later, Girland would come down the stairs and then he would have him.

*   *   *

Girland had heard the door of the banqueting hall ease open. It had opened so gently, Gilly didn't hear it. Girland put his hand on her arm and his left hand touched her lips in a signal to keep silent. He felt her stiffen against him.

He could see nothing in the darkness. His hand closed around the butt of his pistol. He heard the door ease shut.

There was a long pause, then a voice whispered out of the darkness: "Girland ... this is Malik."

For a brief moment Girland was so startled, he remained motionless. Malik! Here? He had immediately recognised the guttural voice.

He pressed Gilly behind him. Then he thumbed back the safety-catch on his gun. The little snick of the catch made a loud noise in the vast silence of the room.

"Don't move," Girland said. "I have a gun in my hand."

"Don't you recognise my voice, Girland?" Malik asked. "You don't need the gun."

Girland snapped on his flashlight. The small, powerful beam hit the double doors, shifted to the right and centred on Malik who was standing against the wall, his hands raised.

Gilly caught her breath at the sight of this giant of a man and she retreated.

Girland lowered the beam of his flashlight so it didn't dazzle Malik.

"You're the last person I expected to see, Comrade," he said. "What are you doing here?"

"It seemed to me," Malik said, "that you needed help."

Girland laughed.

"An understatement." He paused and looked thoughtfully at Malik. "Since when have you wanted to help me?"

"I owe you something."

Girland's puzzled expression cleared.

"I get it ... last time we parted you promised to buy me a drink. Is this your idea of a drink?"

"Call it that if you like. I'm here to help."

Girland walked down the vast room, keeping his flashlight's beam on Malik's legs until he reached him. He put his gun back in his hip pocket and offered his hand.

"It's quite a time ... I've missed you."

The two men shook hands.

"I think I have also missed you," Malik said. "At least when we were fighting against each other, it was amusing. Since last time we met, life hasn't been amusing."

They were speaking so quietly that Gilly who was crouched against the far wall, couldn't hear what they were saying. This silver-haired giant scared her. Seeing Girland walk towards him and then shake hands with him did nothing to allay her fears.

"You'd better meet Gillian Sherman," Girland. said.

They joined Gilly at the far end of the room. With Girland holding the flashlight so they could all see each other, he made the introductions.

"Gilly, I want you to meet an old enemy of mine of the Soviet Intelligence. His name is Malik: a name that is as infamous as it is famous."

Gilly looked at Malik with horror. He regarded her with his flat evil green eyes with the indifference of a man regarding a hole in a wall.

"Malik, this is Gillian Sherman, the daughter of the possible future President of the United States," Girland went on, enjoying himself. "Shake hands nicely and let's be sociable."

Gilly backed away while Malik thrust his hands in his pockets.

"I know all about her," Malik said in German. "I want to talk to you." He paused, then went on, "Can she understand German?"

"No ... French but no German."

189

"Good." Malik took out his flashlight, turned it on and walked halfway down the room. He sat down in one of the high back leather chairs and lit a cigarette.

"He wants to talk to me," Girland said to Gilly. "There's nothing to be scared about. Sit there and wait for me." He led her to a chair against the far wall.

"I'm frightened of that man ... he's evil."

"Just relax. I know a lot more about him than you do." The conversation was carried on in whispers. "Sit down and leave this to me."

"You're so goddamn cocky, aren't you?" Gilly exploded in a furious whisper. "You're so sure of yourself? I tell you he's evil!"

Girland felt for her face, pinched her chin in his forefinger and thumb and kissed her. For a moment she tried to avert her face, then her lips met his and parted.

"Another time ... another place," Girland said, drawing back.

He again turned on his flashlight and made his way to a chair next to the one Malik was sitting in. He sat down beside him.

"Cigarette?" Malik asked, offering his pack.

Girland took the Russian cigarette and both men lit up.

There was a brief pause, then Malik said, speaking in soft German, "I want you to know, Girland, I'm working with you. That's why I'm here."

This statement didn't entirely surprise Girland. He had heard through his various contacts that Malik was out of favour and had been taken out of the active field. He was aware that Malik owed him his life. This man now appeared to be an odd mixture: ruthless, dangerous and clever, but now it seemed there was a sentimental streak in him.

"I remember what you said when last we met," Malik went on from out of the darkness, "that we are professionals and the little stinkers who pull the strings are the amateurs. I've often thought about that. We both have to earn a living, do what we are told ... I much more than you, but there comes a time when it is possible to hit back at the little stinkers. You walked out on Dorey ... I have my chance now to get even with Kovski."

"Comrade Kovski ... how is he?" Girland asked lightly.

"Better than he is going to be," Malik said grimly. "He has given me the assignment to find out why Sherman came to Paris, why Dorey gave you a movie projector and why you have come to Bavaria."

"How are you progressing?"

"Well enough." Malik drew on his cigarette, and for a brief moment the glowing end of the cigarette lit up his square, Slavonic features. "This girl has made a pornographic film. With this film, she is blackmailing her father. She is a member of an anti-war organisation, run by Rosnold, a pornographic photographer who is now dead. Sherman went to Dorey for help. Dorey realised he couldn't make this official so he appealed to you. You followed these two to Garmisch. Somehow Herman Radnitz heard of this. This is his Schloss. You were invited ... you fell for the invitation and now you are trapped here. I followed you here. I saw Rosnold shot. I saw a man leave in Rosnold's car. He is being followed. I climbed over the wall and here I am."

Girland grinned in the darkness.

"Pretty sound work, Malik," he said. "You're right on the beam. The man using Rosnold's car has gone to get the films ... there are three of them. When they have them, they will knock the girl on the head and that will conclude the operation."

"Knock you on the head too?"

"Certain to."

"Why wait? We can leave now," Malik said. "We can get down by the rope. I came up by it. There are three men guarding the lodge at the gates. That is where the switch is operating the current to the walls. You and I could take them easily and we are away. My gun is silenced."

"The girl couldn't get down the rope."

"Does she matter? Why not leave her?"

"No ... besides, there is a slight complication." Girland grinned in the darkness. "I'm not leaving until I get those three films. The girl and I remain here until the messenger returns. He won't be back before 08.00 hrs tomorrow."

"I see. Sherman is paying you of course."

"Why else do you imagine I'm sticking my neck out?"

Malik dropped the butt of his cigarette on the floor and put his foot on it.

"You have always been obsessed by money."

"Aren't you?"

"No ... because in my country you don't have much money ... you don't get the chance to put a value on it. So you will stay here until the films arrive ... then what do you propose to do?"

"Get them and walk out."

"Then what do you propose to do?" Malik repeated, a note of impatience in his voice.

"What I said. I'll stick a gun in the count's well-fed back and make him drive us out of here."

Malik remained silent for a long moment.

"So I have to stay here with you until 08.00 hrs tomorrow?"

"You don't have to."

"I said I would help you. You can't do this on your own with the girl. You need someone to guard your back. A quick shot through the back of your head and the operation fails. There is an expert gunman here. Did you see how he picked off Rosnold? A perfect shot through the head. You wouldn't stand a chance."

Girland rubbed his jaw.

"I'm going to get those films. They are worth ten thousand dollars to me. I'm going to wait for them to arrive."

Malik flashed on his flashlight and looked at his cheap Czech watch. The time was 02.00 hrs.

"Then we have sixteen hours to wait," he said.

"That's about right."

"Without food?"

"I'll get some from downstairs later."

"Don't under-rate that gunman. He is a first-class shot."

Girland stood up.

"So you are sticking with me?"

"Yes."

"I can use you ... thanks. Let's get some sleep. There's a bed in the room next to this one. Sleep lightly."

"I don't need sleep," Malik said curtly. "You take the bed. I'll keep watch."

Girland wasn't going to argue about this. He liked his sleep.

He went down the room to where Gilly was waiting.

"Come on ... we're going back to the four-poster. Malik will keep watch," he said to her.

She followed him silently past Malik. They paused in the doorway, saw the guard was still sleeping at the head of the stairs and slipped silently into the room they had previously occupied. They stretched out on the bed.

"I don't understand," Gilly said as she lay beside Girland. "Is that man really a Russian agent?"

"He's probably the best of all their agents."

"Then what is he doing here?"

"Russia wouldn't welcome your father as President. Don't bother your brains about it. I'm going to sleep."

Gilly half sat up.

"But how could the Russians get to know about me?"

"The Russians always make capital out of reckless and stupid acts," Girland said. "You've handed them something on a plate, but don't bother your brains about it. I'm going to sleep."

He was asleep long before Gilly finally drifted off into an uneasy doze. The hours ticked away. At six-thirty, the first light of the dawn came through the slots in the wooden shutters and Girland came awake.

He yawned, stretched and slid off the bed.

Gilly started up.

"Wait here," he said and moved silently to the door. He eased it open and looked down the long corridor. The guard was gone. He looked towards the double doors of the banqueting room. Malik was sitting in the half-open doorway, smoking.

"The guard left half an hour ago," Malik said softly. "There's a bathroom right opposite. I've been doing a little exploring." He got to his feet and joined Girland.

"Nothing happened?"

Malik shook his head.

"That rope might not bluff them. They could search the whole place."

"We'll wait until they do."

Having made his toilet, Girland returned to the bedroom and led Gilly to the bathroom.

"The guards have gone," he told her. "Go ahead, but be quick."

It was while she was in the bathroom, they heard sounds of activity going on downstairs. Girland went cautiously down the corridor and peered over the banister rail. He could see the fourth and third stair heads. No one was guarding them. He could hear the murmur of voices from the ground floor, but couldn't hear what was being said. He returned to Malik.

Gilly came from the bathroom. In the dim light coming through the shutters, she looked pale and scared.

"They will find the rope pretty soon," Girland said. "Now the staircase isn't guarded, we'll go up to the next floor. They are certain to come up here."

Malik nodded.

The three moved down the corridor, paused at the foot of the staircase leading to the sixth floor, listened, then Girland drawing his gun, went up silently. Edging around the bend in the staircase, he assured himself no one was up there and he signalled for Gilly and Malik to come up.

"We'll wait here and see what happens," he said and sat down on the carpet, his back against the wall, just out of sight of the stair head. The other two joined him. "I could do with a pint of coffee with eggs and lashings of bacon," he went on.

Malik eyed him, but said nothing. He disapproved of such weakness. Gilly grimaced. The thought of food, in her present state of panic, revolted her.

It wasn't until well after 08.00 hrs that they heard a loud voice, speaking in German, come drifting up the well of the stairs. The man was saying: "I want every one of you out into the forest. Take guns! These two must be found! Everyone is to go!"

Girland and Malik exchanged glances, then Girland got to his feet.

"Watch the stairs," he said and moving along the corridor, he opened a door on his right and entered a small unfurnished room with a short spiral staircase, leading to one of the turrets. He climbed the stairs and moved into the turret. The slotted windows gave him a direct view down on the lawn and onto the distant forest.

He waited. Some five minutes later, he saw the first of von Goltz's men coming across the lawn, heading for the forest. He began to count them ... fifteen ... twenty-three ... thirty ... They broke up and formed a long even line, each man ten metres apart from the other. They entered the forest. Girland continued to wait. Another five men came across the lawn, slowly followed by an enormously fat man who Girland guessed would be the chef. He plodded forward slowly, followed by another man who kept waving his arms as he talked to the fat man.

Ten minutes later, Girland saw an estate car full of women drive down to the gates. He watched the gates open and the car move off along the main road to Garmisch. Still he waited. Then he saw von Goltz, carrying a shotgun, with his major-domo at his heels also cross the lawn and enter the forest.

After waiting another ten minutes, Girland decided there was no one else to come and he returned to the corridor where Gilly looked expectantly at him. Malik was leaning over the banister, listening and watching. He straightened when Girland came from the room.

"Well?"

"Thirty-eight men and a number of women have left," Girland said. "The count with his major-domo has also gone into the forest. Did you hear anything?"

"They sent three men up to the room below. They took away the curtain cord and then went down again."

The two men looked at each other.

"This could be a trap," Girland said. "A bluff ... like the rope. The gunman could have been left behind to wait for us to show."

Malik nodded.

"Yes. Shall we go down and find him?"

Gilly listened, her eyes growing round.

"He might not be down there. We'll play it safe just in case he is. We have plenty of time. We'll give him an hour or so. He doesn't know for certain we are up here. Let's stretch his nerves a little."

Again Malik nodded.

"I'll stay here ... you watch from the turret. We want to be sure they don't give up the search in the forest and come back."

"Yes." Girland turned to Gilly. "Come with me." He led her into the turret-room. "I'm going up into the turret. You sit on the floor. You may have a long wait, but try to amuse yourself. Think of all the nice things you've done in your life if you can remember them ... that should keep you occupied."

Gilly flushed.

"There are moments when I could kill you!" she said fiercely. "You treat me like a child!"

"No, Gilly ... not a child."

Girland regarded her for a long moment, then went up the turret stairs.

Gilly choked back a sob. That cool, indifferent look he had given her told her as no words could his opinion of her. What really hurt her was that she knew his opinion of her was the same as her own.

*   *   *

Lu Silk sat motionless in his chair, his gun resting in his lap. The silence in this vast Schloss was depressing, but Silk was used to silence. He was also used to waiting. He was sure, sooner or later, Girland would come down the stairs, and then he would have him.

While he sat there, Silk recalled another long wait he once had – when was it? Three years back? He nodded to himself. Yes, three years back.

There was an agitator, Jack Adams, who was stirring up trouble among the men working on one of Radnitz's big building projects. The work was slowing down and Radnitz could see he could get caught on the compensation clause: big money, so he had given Silk the signal to get rid of Adams.

Adams had lived in a two-room walk-up in Brooklyn. He knew he was in danger, but he had a lot of confidence in himself which was a mistake when dealing with a man like Silk.

Silk had rented a room across the road, facing Adams' apartment block. He arrived there early one morning and took up a position on the hard kitchen chair, the curtains of the window half drawn. He had brought with him his favourite killing weapon: a .22 target rifle with a telescopic sight. He waited for Adams to show. He wasn't to know that Adams was in bed with flu. There was an important mass meeting being held at 21.00 hrs that evening and Radnitz had ordered Silk to stop Adams from attending. Silk imagined Adams was certain to go out during the day, so he waited. He waited for thirteen hours. He hadn't brought food with him, and around 17.00 hrs he was hungry, thirsty and viciously angry. He didn't dare leave the window for a second. He knew that when Adams moved, he always moved fast, and his shabby car was parked only a few yards from the entrance to the apartment block.

Sitting in his chair, now waiting for Girland, Silk told himself the Adams affair had been the longest endurance test he had ever had, but it had taught him that if you wait long enough, were patient enough, you fixed what you were hired to fix.

Adams had finally shown at 20.30 hrs. The light was bad and he moved fast, running down the steps and heading for his car.

Because Silk hadn't relaxed for a moment during those long thirteen hours, he was ready for him. As Adams paused briefly to unlock the car door, Silk got his head in the centre of the cross hairs of the telescopic sight and squeezed the trigger. That had been the end of Adams' trouble making.

Because of this experience, Silk was prepared to wait all day for Girland. The count would keep his men out in the forest until dusk. Sooner or later, Girland would make his break. The success or failure of this trap depended on whether Girland believed the Schloss had been evacuated. If he suspected a trap, then he might remain out of sight in spite of hunger and thirst. Although he was unarmed, there were plenty of weapons to hand ... swords, knives, battle-axes that adorned most of the walls, but these kind of weapons didn't bother Silk. He knew no man born could compete with him with a hand weapon against his gun.

Silk would have liked to smoke, but that would be a give-away. He crossed one leg over the other and relaxed, his ears pricked and his one eye on the half open door.

In the big hall was a splendid grandfather clock. During the steady swing of its pendulum, the lead weight slightly touched the case of the clock, making a distinct and regular noise. After half an hour of listening to this noise, Silk found it was getting on his nerves. He wanted to go out into the hall and stop the clock, but this would be too dangerous. If Girland was somewhere upstairs, he too could hear the scrape ... scrape ... scrape from the clock, and he would be immediately alerted if the clock was stopped.

The clock suddenly struck nine: its soft mellow chimes startling Silk. Later, it startled him again when it struck ten. Although he imagined he had nerves of steel, he found the two hour wait had made him too tense. Twice during this time, he imagined he had heard another slight sound above the scraping of the pendulum and he had half-risen to his feet. Then satisfied that Girland wasn't creeping down the stairs, he sat back, his hand closing over his pack of cigarettes, then remembering, had silently cursed. He was now longing for a cigarette. At least, during those thirteen hours when he had waited for Adams, he had smoked incessantly.

He began to think of Girland. This man was a trained CIA agent. Silk's thin mouth formed into a wry grimace. His first murder assignment had been against a CIA agent, a man who had collected enough evidence to put Radnitz behind bars and had to be eliminated immediately.*

In those days, Silk had been very sure of himself: too sure. The agent had been almost too quick for him and had shot him in the face. Although he had finally managed to kill the agent, he had to spend six months in hospital and had come out with only one eye.

The experience had left him with a subconscious dread of facing another CIA man. But during his years with Radnitz, his victims had been easy ... pigeons, to be shot down without means, training or guts to protect themselves.

* see *Believed Violent*, by James Hadley Chase

Radnitz had warned him about Girland. As he sat in the chair, he remembered von Goltz's consternation. Are you quite sure you shouldn't have two or three of my men with you?

Silk touched his forehead with the back of his hand. It infuriated him to find he was sweating.

The grandfather clock in the hall began to strike eleven.

*　　　*　　　*

Girland came down the turret stairs. For three weary, boring hours he had been watching the forest without seeing any of von Goltz's men.

"Gilly ... make yourself useful. Go up in the turret and watch the forest. If you see anyone coming back, let me know. I want to talk to Malik."

He left her and joined Malik in the corridor.

"I think it's time to start something," he said, keeping his voice low. "You've heard nothing?"

"No."

"We could be wasting time. They may have completely evacuated the place, but I'm not taking chances. The gunman could still be here, waiting. If he's anywhere, he'll be in the main living-room. It's only from the door of that room you have a clear view of the stairs. I want to make sure he is there. I'm going down by the rope."

Malik shook his head.

"It's too risky. You can't climb down without making some noise. If he hears you, he'll come out onto the terrace and you're a dead duck." He paused for a moment, then went on, "How far can you go down the stairs without being seen?"

"To the third floor."

"Then let's go down. It's time to put pressure on his nerves," Malik said. "I'll go out onto one of the balconies and start tapping on the balcony rail. It's a trick I've used before, and it worked."

This made sense to Girland. He nodded.

"What do I do?"

"Stay at the head of the stairs. If I spot him come out on the terrace, I'll rap twice quickly. If you move fast, you can get down to the second floor before he gets back."

"Right."

Both men drew their guns and moved down the stairs. Both of them were trained to move like ghosts and they reached the third floor landing without a sound.

While Girland remained by the stair head, Malik moved down the corridor. He spent some moments easing open one of the doors inch by inch until he had enough space to slide into the room. The shutters across the windows presented a problem. Would they creak when he opened them? With infinite patience he unlatched and opened the shutters. The operation took nearly five minutes but he got them open without a sound. He stepped onto the balcony and saw that the big windows of the main living-room were below and to his right. He lay flat on the balcony where he could peer through the balcony rails, yet squirm back instantly out of sight.

Using the barrel of his gun, he began to tap on the lower rung of the balcony rail. The silence, hanging over the Schloss, accentuated the sound.

He tapped at irregular intervals. Tap-tap-tap. A long pause; then tap-tap-tap-tap.

Silk heard the sound and stiffened to attention. He looked swiftly behind him as the sound came from that direction.

He came out of his chair like a cat, gun in hand. Standing motionless, listening, he looked what he was: a vicious, professional killer. The tapping sound stopped, and there was silence, except for the scrape-scrape-scrape from the grandfather clock.

A bird? Silk wondered. Water dripping?

He waited, listened, then decided the sound was of no importance. He wiped his sweating face savagely with the back of his hand and again longed for a cigarette.

Minutes dragged by. The pendulum of the clock continued its soft irritating sound.

Then the tapping began again.

Silk looked out onto the sunlit terrace. A branch of a tree? No. The sound was too metallic for that. The sound was coming from outside. Silk moved to the open French windows.

The tapping continued. Silk was now certain it was coming from the terrace. Someone out there? A trap? He edged closer to the window, paused to look back and through the half open door where he could see the stairs: nothing moved out there.

The tapping stopped, and again silence closed in around Silk. He edged further forward. Nothing happened. He felt a surge of rage run through him, aware that he was jumpy and his nerves were crawling. Then just when he was deciding to return to his chair, the tapping began again.

He remembered von Goltz had assured him that Girland was unarmed. He decided he had to investigate this sound. Moving like a black shadow, he stepped out onto the terrace, his gun ready.

Malik saw him and tapped twice fast, then squirmed back out of sight.

Girland heard the two quick taps and went down the stairs, fast and silently to the second floor. Now he could see the half open door leading into the living-room and caught a glimpse of the empty chair, pulled near the doorway. He stepped back into the corridor.

Silk looked up at the rows of balconies above him. He saw nothing suspicious. His nerves were now so taut that he became reckless with rage. He stepped right out onto the terrace where he had a good view of the balconies.

Malik grinned and lifted his pistol. It was a difficult shot as the bars of the balcony obstructed his view.

Silk saw the movement although he didn't see the pistol. He fired instantly. The bullet slammed against the concrete just below Malik's head, spraying splinters, one of which hit Malik across the bridge of his nose. He started back, and Silk, now knowing where his opponent was, dashed back into the living-room.

He had had enough of this cat and mouse business. He knew Girland had no gun and he knew he was on the third floor. He didn't hesitate. Rushing across the hall, he went up the stairs two at the time, not caring about the noise he was making.

In the corridor on the second floor, Girland heard him coming and quickly stepped into a nearby room.

Silk came pounding up the stairs. As he started up the next flight of stairs, Girland went after him. Halfway up the stairs, Silk heard him. He stopped short and spun around, but Girland was on him, grabbing at his ankles. Girland heaved and Silk went over his head to crash down the stairs, his gun flying out of his hand.

Girland spun around and launched himself at Silk as Silk was struggling to his feet. Silk couldn't avoid the flying body and went down under Girland with a crash that set the weapons on the walls jangling.

With strength that startled Girland, Silk threw him off and the two men rolled apart. Girland was first into action.

He was half up and slamming himself down on Silk before Silk could raise himself. Girland chopped with the side of his hand, smashing down on the side of Silk's neck. Silk went out like a snuffed candle.

Malik came leaping down the stairs as Girland bent over Silk. Seeing the blood on Malik's face, Girland asked, "You hurt?"

"It's nothing." Malik wiped his face with his handkerchief. He stared down at Silk. "Who is he?"

"I wouldn't know ... sweet looking specimen, isn't he? You watch him. I'll get a curtain cord."

Girland went into one of the rooms and broke off a length of cord. He returned and bound Silk's hands behind his back and his ankles together.

"Let's dump him out of the way."

They carried Silk's unconscious body into the room and put him on a bed.

"He'll be out for an hour or so." Girland tore off a piece of the dustsheet covering the bed and gagged Silk. "Let's hunt up some food ... I'm starving. Hang on a moment, I'll get Gilly."

Ten minutes later, the three of them were sitting in the vast kitchen, hungrily eating cold chicken and thick slices of ham.

"I have an idea," Malik said as he began to demolish another slice of ham. "We don't have to stay here until the messenger arrives. We can meet him at the Munich airport. Between the two of us we can persuade him to part with the films. We could be back in Paris by midnight."

"Too risky. We might not spot the messenger."

"I had a good look at him ... I'll spot him."

"How about the electric fence?"

Malik wiped his mouth with the back of his hand.

"We'll take a car ... there are four of them in the garage, go down to the lodge, take it, turn off the current and we're on our way."

Girland considered this idea. He checked his watch. The next plane from Paris wouldn't arrive for another five hours. They had plenty of time.

"Okay ... we'll do it." He turned to Gilly. "Can you drive, baby?"

"Of course ... and don't call me baby!"

Girland laughed.

"Come on up and pack." He turned to Malik. "Will you get the car?"

Ten minutes later, Girland, carrying Gilly's bag and his own, followed by Gilly, ran down the steps to the waiting white Mercedes 200.

"You drive," Girland said to Gilly as he dumped the bags in the boot of the car.

He and Malik got in the back. Gilly set the car in motion and drove down the long, twisting drive until Girland told her to stop.

"We'll go the rest of the way on foot. When I whistle, come on down to the gates."

"Please be careful!" Gilly said. She was getting scared again.

"Oh, sure ... just relax and listen for my whistle."

He joined Malik, and together they went swiftly on down the drive. When in sight of the lodge, they paused.

"I'll go around the back," Malik said, drawing his gun. "Give me a couple of minutes."

But they need not have taken precautions for the three guards in the lodge were having lunch. They were absorbed in a vast meal of white sausages with a mustard sauce and sauerkraut.

Girland kicked open the door and the three guards stared with stupefied eyes at his threatening gun. Malik joined him.

"Turn the current off!" Malik snarled and the threat of his green eyes so scared the head guard that he scrambled to his feet and pulled down a lever on the wall.

It took them a few minutes to tie each man securely to his chair, then Malik and Girland left the lodge.

While Malik ran to open the big gates, Girland went up the drive and whistled piercingly.

Later, as Girland drove the Mercedes into the crowded car park at the Munich airport, Gilly said, "There's the TR4." She pointed to where the scarlet TR4 was parked among other cars.

Malik, sitting in the back of the Mercedes, leaned forward.

"I'll handle this," he said. "The messenger may have seen you. He hasn't seen me. Here's what we do …"

*   *   *

As the aircraft from Paris stopped at the arrival bay, Fritz Kirst reluctantly undid his safety belt. He wasn't pleased to be back, but it had certainly been marvellous luck to have been sent to Paris on such an easy mission. When he had arrived, the bank had been closed so he had the whole evening and half the night to explore this city which he had never had the good fortune to visit before.

Kirst had only been working for von Goltz for two years. He had a badly paid job as an assistant to the estate manager who constantly bullied him. Kirst was far from satisfied with his job and was planning to make a change as soon as something better came along. However, the Paris trip had made up for a lot of his past grievances, and although he had spent more money than he could afford, he told himself, as he walked through the Customs, that it had been worth it.

A silver-haired giant of a man approached him.

"Your name?"

The snap in the voice and the cold green eyes brought Kirst to attention. He was so used to being snapped at by his superiors he reacted automatically.

"Fritz Kirst, sir," he said.

Malik nodded.

"Good ... your master told me to pick you up. Follow me," and without looking at Kirst, Malik, knowing the German weakness for obeying orders, turned on his heel and walked briskly to where the Mercedes was parked.

Kirst, a little bewildered, had to break into a trot to keep up with him. Who was this man? he was asking himself. Why had the count sent him? But when he saw the count's car, his uneasiness disappeared. Malik was already at the wheel, and Kirst had to scramble in as Malik eased the car out of the parking bay.

As Malik drove out onto the main road, Kirst said timidly, "Excuse me, sir, but ... "

"I don't like people talking to me when I'm driving!" Malik snapped.

Kirst placed his briefcase on his knees and sat back, snubbed and silent.

This big man certainly could handle a car, he thought as Malik whipped the Mercedes through the traffic with expert ease. They quickly left Munich behind. As they reached the highway to Garmisch, Kirst happened to look in the offside wing mirror. He stared ... stared again, then stiffened.

Right behind the Mercedes was a small scarlet car. Kirst immediately recognised the driver and the girl beside him.

They were the two the count was keeping prisoners at the Schloss, and that car! It was the car he had been ordered to leave at the airport!

Sweat broke out on his face. He looked wildly at Malik who glared at him so evilly Kirst shuddered.

"Sit still and keep quiet!" Malik snarled.

Some way down the busy highway, there was a left turn: a narrow country road leading to a distant farmhouse. Malik slowed, swung the car down the road, drove until he reached a bend that would put the car out of sight from the highway and pulled up.

"You have a packet from a Paris bank I want," Malik said. "Give it to me!"

The TR4 pulled up behind the Mercedes and Girland slid out. He came to the offside door of the Mercedes and looked through the open window at Kirst.

"Has he given it to you?"

"Not yet ... but he will."

Kirst hesitated for only a second, then with shaking hands, he opened the briefcase and took from it a square-shaped, sealed packet. Malik took it from him and examined it.

Girland quietly slid his gun from his hip pocket. He didn't trust Malik. He kept the gun down by his side, but the movement hadn't escaped Malik who looked up, stared at him and grinned.

"You take after me ... you trust nobody," he said and reaching across Kirst, he thrust the packet at Girland who took it with his left hand.

"I apologise ... force of habit," Girland said and put the gun back into his hip pocket. He went over to Gilly who was waiting in the TR4. "Is this it?" he asked showing her the packet.

"Yes," Gilly said and made a quick snatch at it, but Girland was too quick for her. She looked pleadingly at him. "Please give it to me ... it's mine!"

Girland shook his head.

"Don't let's go all over this again, Gilly. You gave me your word. This goes to your father."

She went white.

"No! Please! I couldn't live knowing he had seen those films! If you give them to him, I'll kill myself! I swear I will!"

Girland studied her.

"But, Gilly, shouldn't you have thought of this before you made them? After all, you were going to send them to his enemies, weren't you?"

"Of course not! Please believe me! I was bluffing. Of course I wasn't going to send them to them. I can't bear to think of anyone seeing them!"

"Oh come on, Gilly. You've already sent one spool to your father."

"I didn't! It was Pierre! He sent it and then told me afterwards! I could have killed him! Besides, these ..." She caught her breath in a sob. "They – they are much worse. I can't bear anyone seeing them. Don't you understand? I didn't know what I was doing as you or anyone else wouldn't have if you had had as much LSD as I had." Tears began to run down her face. "You can't do this to me!"

Girland regarded the packet in his hand, then looked at her.

"This little lot is worth ten thousand dollars to me. Why should I care what it does to you?"

She hid her face in her hands and began to sob violently, rocking herself to and fro: a picture of misery. Girland became aware that Malik had got out of the Mercedes and was watching him curiously.

Still holding the packet in his hand, Girland said, "What are we going to do with our friend?"

"Tie him up and dump him here," Malik said. "Someone will find him. It'll give us time to get back to the airport and catch the Paris plane if we hurry."

Girland looked at Gilly who was rocking herself backwards and forwards and he shook his head.

"Gilly ... cut the act. It's good, but it doesn't convince me. You are like a lot of people ... when they are on top, they're fine. When the cards fall wrong, they snivel. I don't believe Rosnold was behind this. I think you were and now, without him, you've lost your guts. Here ... take them." He placed the packet on the hood of the TR4. Turning, he went to the Mercedes and took from the boot, Gilly's suitcase. This he dropped behind the driving seat of the TR4. Gilly continued to sob, her face hidden in her hands. Girland regarded her, grimaced, then shrugged. He walked back to the Mercedes.

"Let's drive further up the road to the next bend," he said, getting into the car.

"You're forgetting the packet," Malik said as he slid under the driving wheel.

"Don't be so obvious, Comrade," Girland said. "Let's move."

Malik drove to the next bend and then pulled up. He told Kirst to get out. While he was tying Kirst's trembling hands behind his back, Girland lit a cigarette. He heard the TR4 start up.

Malik looked at him.

"She's going."

"Yes."

"She's taken the packet."

"Yes."

Malik tied Kirst's ankles together, then picking him up, dropped him over the hedge.

"I thought you were interested in money, Girland," he said. "Wasn't Dorey going to pay you for those films?"

"So he said." Girland got into the passenger's seat of the car. "Come on … let's move."

With a puzzled expression, Malik started the car, reversed and headed down to the highway.

Although Malik drove fast, Girland saw no sign of the scarlet TR4. Gilly was driving even faster.

*   *   *

There were only six other passengers on the last flight to Paris and Girland and Malik sat together, away from the others.

Both men were silent: both occupied with their thoughts.

Girland said suddenly, "You won't tell me unless you want to, Malik, but there's no harm in asking. Just why did you give up those films? I was anticipating trouble. With them, you could have made a big hit with your people. They wouldn't have hesitated to use them and Sherman would have been sunk. Have you lost interest in your work?"

Malik stared broodingly down at his big hands. For some moments, Girland thought he wasn't going to reply, then he said, "At last I'm following your example. Ever since I began working for security, I've never considered my own interests whereas you have always put yourself first and your job second. Now I've decided to do just that. As long as Kovski is in power, I will never be allowed to return to the active field where I belong. Sitting at a desk, handling paper is death to me. This is my chance to destroy Kovski and I am taking it. Once he is destroyed, I will get back to the active field." He turned his head and his flat green eyes searched Girland's face. "Then you and I will be enemies again."

"Maybe we won't meet again," Girland said, shrugging. "It's only because Dorey keeps tempting me with money that I fall for his cockeyed assignments. He may get tired of it. How are you fixing Comrade Kovski?"

Again Malik took his time before answering. Finally, he said, "When I report tomorrow, I will tell him you destroyed the films before I could get them. I will remind him that if he had acted on my suggestion and had cabled the American airport police that Sherman was returning on a false passport, Sherman would have been ruined by now ... that the films meant nothing. We could have prevented Sherman becoming President by sending this cable. This Kovski stupidly refused to do. I will then tell him that a tape recording of our conversation is on its way to Moscow." Malik looked down at his hands and smiled evilly. "That will be the moment ... when he realises what I have done ... that I shall enjoy."

Girland nodded.

"I can imagine. Dorey will be pleased."

Malik shrugged his heavy shoulders.

"Many people will be pleased." He looked at his watch. "We will be landing in a few minutes. We must not be seen together. Drina will be on duty at the airport. Will you go first? I will follow after you when Drina is telephoning that you are back."

"That's okay."

As the plane began its descent, Malik looked directly at Girland.

"I'll say goodbye now. I hope we don't meet again. In a couple of months I'll be back in the active field. We are all square now ... you understand?"

Girland laughed.

"I can take a hint. I hope we don't meet again and thanks for your help. Yes ... we're all square."

He offered his hand and Malik gripped it, then as the plane touched down and began to taxi towards the arrival bay, both men unfastened their safety belts.

*　　*　　*

Girland was disappointed when he walked into Dorey's outer office to find Mavis Paul not at her desk.

He flicked down the switch on the intercom connecting with Dorey's office.

"Yes?" Dorey's voice asked.

"This is your favourite ex-agent reporting," Girland said. "Did I wake you up?"

"Oh ... you. Come in."

Girland entered the big room, sauntered across to the visitor's chair and sank into it. He was wearing a lightweight grey tweed suit, a blood-red tie and dark-brown casuals. Dorey was surprised to see him so well turned out.

"Nice to see me again?" Girland asked with a jeering little smile.

Dorey regarded him over the tops of his spectacles.

"Did you get those films?"

Girland lifted his shoulders. He took his time before saying, "Yes and no. I did have them, but the poor little girl sobbed so hard when I told her I was giving them to her old man that I gave them back to her."

Dorey stiffened.

"Are you trying to waste my time?"

"I wouldn't dream of doing that. If you don't believe me, call up the Soviet Embassy and ask Malik. Without him, I doubt if I would have got the films. He was an eye-witness to the touching scene when I decided, not without pain to myself, that I would rather let the girl have them than her creep of a father."

"In other words you haven't the films ... you have failed," Dorey exclaimed, his face flushing with anger.

"I didn't fail. I don't fail. I got them and you can assure your pal that he can go ahead and run for office. The films have been destroyed. Gillian has promised to behave herself in the future. You can't call that failure, can you?"

"Do you expect me to believe any of this?" Dorey said furiously. "Your assignment was to bring those films to me! Now stop this fooling! Have you got them or haven't you?"

"I know you are getting old, but I didn't realise you are also getting deaf, Dorey," Girland said, looking sad. "The girl has destroyed them. She has promised to leave her father strictly alone in the future."

"How do I know she has destroyed them? A promise from a slut like that? What is that worth?" Dorey demanded, banging his fist on the desk.

"Did you know Sherman gave the green light to Radnitz to have her murdered?" Girland asked quietly.

Dorey stiffened and looked hard at Girland who had lost his bantering expression. There was a steely gleam in his eyes that told Dorey he was being deadly serious.

"I think you should tell me just what has been happening," he said.

"I'll tell you ... that's why I'm here. By the way, how has your pal Sherman been getting along since I've been away?"

"What do you expect? Because of his daughter, he has had to remain at home. He's lost ground. You can't fight an election at home."

Girland brightened.

"Well, that's good news. Perhaps Gilly has struck a mortal blow after all."

"I'm not saying that, but he is now behind. Ten days are vital at this period of the election."

"So the creep might not become President after all?"

"Never mind about him. What's been happening?"

Girland took one of Dorey's cigarettes, lit it and settled himself comfortably. He then proceeded to give Dorey a lucid report of the past events.

Dorey sat in his chair, his chin resting on his fingertips, his eyes hooded as he listened. When Girland described Rosnold's murder, Dorey's lips tightened, but he still didn't interrupt.

"And so when the girl started to cry her eyes out," Girland concluded, "I thought the gentlemanly thing to do was to give her the films ... so I gave them to her. Perhaps you wouldn't have?"

Dorey brooded for some moments.

"You have no real proof that Sherman is implicated with this kidnapping and murder?" he asked finally.

"I don't need proof. Sherman and Radnitz are buddy-buddies. Gilly made a nuisance of herself ... QED. What's it matter anyway? She isn't charging the creep with attempted murder."

Dorey winced.

"I find this difficult to believe," he said slowly, but his shocked eyes told Girland he did believe.

"You don't have to ... it's over now ... who cares?"

"What has happened to the girl?"

Girland shrugged.

"You don't have to worry about her. She is capable of taking care of herself. She'll keep her promise … I'm sure of that."

Dorey began to relax.

"You realise, Girland, that unless I give those three films to Sherman, he won't part with any more money?"

"I knew that when I gave Gilly the films," Girland said and smiled wryly. "I earned the first ten thousand dollars so I keep them but I intend to spend them as fast as I can. I wouldn't take any more money from Sherman if he offered it to me … some money smells, but his money stinks."

Dorey lifted his hands a little helplessly.

"There are times when I don't understand you," he said. "I was under the impression any money smelt good to you."

"Well, we all live and learn." Girland laughed. "I have another choice item of news for you," and he went on to tell Dorey that Kovski was heading for disgrace.

Dorey considered this, then shook his head.

"It isn't good news, Girland. I would rather have a blustering fool like Kovski in charge of Security than a devil like Malik back in the active field. You're not using your head."

Girland acknowledged the truth of this by nodding.

"Yes … I must admit that fact had escaped me. Not that I could have done anything about it. It's Malik's private vendetta. Anyway, it doesn't matter to me. I'm distinctly ex now. I don't suppose I'll ever run into Malik again. You had better warn your boys. They have been having it too soft recently."

Dorey rubbed his jaw as he regarded Girland.

"I don't believe you really want to leave us, Girland. Now there is an interesting little job in Tangier that would exactly suit you." He reached for a file and drew it lovingly towards him. "Plenty of action ... two women ... pretty ones involved. Yes, it would exactly suit you and I know you could handle it."

Girland lifted his eyebrows.

"The old siren at work again. How about the money?"

"This is an official job so you would be paid official rates," Dorey said, a sudden waspish note in his voice.

Girland levered himself out of the chair.

"No, thank you. I have ten thousand dollars to squander. I've given up working for peanuts." He lifted his hand and flapped his fingers at Dorey. "So long. If anything crops up in the ten thousand dollar bracket, I might consider it. Think big is my motto: should be yours too."

He wandered out, closing the door gently behind him. His face lit up with his charming smile as he saw Mavis Paul at her typewriter.

She looked up, flushed and then continued to type.

"Not a word of welcome?" Girland said, coming to the desk and smiling down at her. "Not one glad little cry of pleasure?"

Mavis hesitated and then stopped typing. She looked up at him.

"Did anyone tell you you have eyes like stars and lips made for a kiss?" Girland asked. "I got that off a bottle of perfume."

"The exit is behind you and to the right," Mavis said without sounding very convincing.

"How about a dinner with me at Lasserre: soft music, beautiful food, velvety wines? I have lots of money I want to get rid of. Shall we say nine o'clock?"

Mavis regarded him. She thought he looked very handsome. An evening out with him couldn't fail to be exciting. She suddenly realised her life up to now had been all work and no play.

"Thank you ... yes ..."

"My mother once told me that if I didn't at first succeed ..." Girland laughed happily. "This is going to be the most maddeningly exciting evening of my life ... and your life. Then nine o'clock at Lasserre."

She nodded and began typing again.

Girland wandered to the door. As he was about to leave, she stopped typing. He turned and looked inquiringly at her.

Her eyes were sparkling as she asked, "Do you still own that Bukhara rug?"

James Hadley Chase

An Ace Up My Sleeve

When three very different people come together, all out for the same thing and prepared to go to any lengths to get it, the stakes are likely to be high. But, for a wealthy middle-aged woman, an international lawyer and a young American, games of bluff and counter-bluff quickly develop into a dangerous and deadly battle. As the action hots up, Chase weaves a fast-moving story of blackmail, intrigue and extortion with a hair-raising climax.

The Fast Buck

International jewel thief, Paul Hater, knows a secret that everyone wants to know – and will go to any lengths to uncover. How long can he remain silent?

When Hater is arrested in possession of a stolen necklace, the police use every possible means to persuade him to reveal the location of the rest of the collection. He remains silent and so begins his twenty-year prison sentence. Having exhausted all their leads, the International Detective Agency, acting on behalf of the insurers, must patiently await Hater's release before they can hope to find out more. But just as his day of release approaches, Hater is kidnapped by a ruthless international gang determined to force the secret from him and prepared to go to any lengths to do so…

James Hadley Chase

Have a Change of Scene

Larry Carr is a diamond expert in need of a break. So when his psychiatrist suggests he has a change of scene, he jumps at the opportunity to move to Luceville, a struggling industrial town, and become a social worker. This, he thinks, will give him all the rest he needs...until he runs into Rhea Morgan, a ruthless, vicious thief who also happens to be extremely attractive. He falls headlong into the criminal world and embarks upon a thrilling, rapid and dastardly adventure in true Hadley Chase style.

Just a Matter of Time

An old lady's will seems to be causing quite a stir. Suddenly everyone wants to get in on the action, everyone that is, including a master forger, a hospital nurse, a young delinquent, a bank executive and, to make matters worse, a professional killer. With such ingredients, a showdown seems inevitable and James Hadley Chase adds enough suspense to keep you guessing right up to the very last page.

JAMES HADLEY CHASE

MY LAUGH COMES LAST

Farrell Brannigan, President of the National Californian Bank, is an extremely successful man. So when he builds another bank in an up-and-coming town on the Pacific coast, he is given worldwide publicity, and this new bank is hailed as 'the safest bank in the world'. But Brannigan's success came at a price and he made many enemies on his way up the ladder. It seems that one of them is now set on revenge and determined to destroy both the bank and Brannigan himself.

YOU'RE DEAD WITHOUT MONEY

Joey Luck and his daughter Cindy were small-time criminals going nowhere fast...until they joined forces with Vin Pinna, a hardened criminal on the run from Miami. They began to set their sights higher and turned their hands to kidnapping. But their hostage, ex-movie star Don Elliot, seemed to have different ideas. He wanted in so they formed a 'quartet in crime' and this time the stakes were higher still – eight Russian stamps worth a million dollars.

'realistic and suspenseful' – *Observer*

Printed in Great Britain
by Amazon

27759790R00126